D0393778

DISCARD

WASATCH COUNTY LIBRARY
465 EAST 1200 SOUTH
HEBER CITY, UT 84032

# Midway to Heaven

# Midway to Heaven

A Novel by Dean Hughes

DESERET
BOOK

SALT LAKE CITY, UTAH

WASATCH COUNTY LIBRARY
465 EAST 1200 SOUTH
HEBER CITY, UT 84032

© 2004 Dean Hughes

All rights reserved. No part of this book may be reproduced in any form or by any means without permission in writing from the publisher, Deseret Book Company, P. O. Box 30178, Salt Lake City, Utah 84130. This work is not an official publication of The Church of Jesus Christ of Latter-day Saints. The views expressed herein are the responsibility of the author and do not necessarily represent the position of the Church or of Deseret Book Company.

DESERET BOOK is a registered trademark of Deseret Book Company.

Visit us at deseretbook.com

**Library of Congress Cataloging-in-Publication Data**

Hughes, Dean, 1943-
    Midway to heaven / Dean Hughes.
        p.      cm.
    ISBN 1-59038-228-5 (alk. paper)
    1. Mormon families—Fiction.   2. Fathers and daughters—Fiction.   3. Mate selection—Fiction.   I. Title.
    PS3558.U36 M53 2003
    813'.54—dc22                                                              2003019946

Printed in the United States of America                             72876-7174
Quebecor World Book Services, Fairfield, PA

10  9    8    7    6    5    4    3    2    1

For Emily Watts, editor and friend

# Chapter One

Ned Stevens had already gone for a long run and it was not yet eight o'clock in the morning. His goal was to run to the top of Snake Creek Canyon, but today he had settled for pushing a hundred yards or so past his previous high, which he figured was over halfway up the canyon. It was a hard climb, but after he had made the descent and gotten a second wind, he felt so strong that he looped around the golf course at Wasatch Mountain State Park and then took the long route back to his house. His sweats were damp when he reached home even though it was a cool November morning. He did some exercises in his garage and then entered the house through the downstairs door. As he climbed the stairs to the main floor, his legs felt weak, but he liked that sensation. The day had hardly begun and he had already paid the price—pain for gain.

By the time he reached his bedroom, the phone was ringing, so he grabbed the phone by his bed. "Dad," he heard on the other end of the line, "sorry to call so early, but—"

"*Early?* It's the middle of the day. I've been out for my morning run already." Ned sat down on the chair by his bed. He pulled the laces loose on his running shoes.

"Dad, you need to relax a little. You could sleep in once in a while."

"I tried that once—but I didn't like it. Hey, when are you coming home?" He grabbed the heels of his shoes and, one by one, slipped them off.

Ned's daughter, Liz, was a student at Brigham Young University, but she wasn't very far away. Ned lived in the little town of Midway, in Heber Valley, about thirty miles from campus. Liz was the only one of his children who was planning to be home for Thanksgiving.

"I'll be home tomorrow afternoon," Liz said, "but I've got to pull a marathon tonight. I have a big test on the last day before Thanksgiving break—if you can believe it."

"Hey, that's rotten. Why do these professors expect you to study? Don't they know you have things to do?"

"It's not funny, Dad. It's a dirty trick. We only meet two days this week, so a lot of the professors give tests on those days—just to keep us from taking off for the whole week."

"And if they didn't, they'd have to give the tests after the break. Then you'd be mad that they made you study over the holiday."

"That's *exactly* right. I would. But my English professor is doing something even worse. She assigned us a *paper* that's due right after we get back. So I have to work on that this weekend."

"It sounds like a conspiracy. Those people are out to *get* you."

"They *are*, Dad. They're ruining my weekend from both ends."

Ned laughed. He leaned back in his chair and stretched his legs out in front of him. "I'm really proud that you're getting such a great education, Liz. You've learned to be so logical."

"Be quiet. I'm pretty, so I don't have to be logical. That's the deal the world makes. And as far as I'm concerned, it's a good one."

"You're not so pretty as *you* think. You're—"

"*Daaaaadddd.* I'm just kidding. I actually look horrible right now. I never should have cut my hair so short, and I just found out I've been using the wrong color of lipstick my whole life. I looked at one of those charts that—"

"You didn't let me finish, Liz. What I was going to say was, you're not as pretty as *you* think. You're as pretty as *I* think. Or in other words, you're *beautiful.*"

There was quiet on the line for a time. "Dad, you're so sweet," she finally said. "Are you doing okay?"

"Sure. I'm fine. But I can't wait to have you home for a few days. You haven't been here for three weeks."

"I'm anxious to get home too. But the reason I called, I was wondering, would you mind if I bring a friend with me? I feel sorry for the students who can't get home for Thanksgiving and don't have family in Utah."

"Well . . . that would be okay, I guess. But I have some things I want to talk to you about. I was hoping we could have time for that."

"We will. David needs to study. You and I can take a walk or something."

"Who's David?"

"My friend. The one I'm bringing home. He's from Connecticut."

"I thought you were talking about a girl."

"No. I didn't say that."

Now Ned really wished he had said no. This was different. "But I have a fun weekend planned. It's so warm, I thought we could still get in a game of golf on Wednesday, and then I wanted you to help me with my Christmas shopping on Friday."

"We can do that. And if David has to study, we'll leave him home. But he plays golf. He'll probably want to play with us."

"Who is this guy?"

"He's in my ward. He's really nice. I think you're going to like him."

*Whoa! What was that I just heard?*

Ned thought he had picked up a slightly elevated level of enthusiasm in Liz's usually mellow voice, and that frightened him. "Have you been going out with him?"

"Not much. He studies so hard that he doesn't find time to date. He's more the kind of guy you just hang out with. We're buddies, mostly. Anyway, he's a great guy to talk with. He knows something about *everything*. And he's a good listener. You can tell him all your old stories and he won't fall asleep the way I do."

"Couldn't he maybe—"

"Anyway, I just wanted to let you know that I can't head up there until after my test and after David gets finished. So it might be kind of late in the afternoon when we get to Midway."

"Couldn't this David stay somewhere else?"

"Not that I know of, Dad. But don't fuss about him. Really. You're going to like him. And you don't need to clean the house."

"But he must know someone else besides you."

"He'll be fun. Honest. And you and I will still have plenty of time to talk things over. We'll do one of our late-night soul-baring sessions, if we have to, and this time I won't bother you with all my failed romance stories. We'll just talk about whatever

4

you have on your mind. But I'm worried about the way you sound, Dad. Are you going through a bad time again?"

"No. Not at all. I just need a sounding board sometimes."

"I'm not sure I'm wise enough to give you any advice, Dad."

"You don't have to be wise. Mostly, I just need to say some things out loud—to hear how they sound to someone else."

"Boy, what a reversal this is. Remember the talks we used to have when I was in high school—when I'd get all upset about some stupid thing?"

"Some stupid *boy*, usually."

"Oh, I know. Remember Cameron Crandall?"

Ned laughed. "Sure. The entire soap opera. The on-again, off-again romance."

"But he was *so* cute."

"And had such a *cool* car."

Liz had a low, resonant voice that sounded lovely when she talked, but when she laughed she sounded like a seal barking. She was making that sound now. "Yeah. That *was* a factor," she said.

"What I remember is the night you found out you lost the election for student-body president. You cried half the night."

"Oh, I know. And you stayed up with me. That whole thing still makes me mad. It was the girls who wouldn't vote for me. They talk about being equal, but when it comes right down to it . . . oh, never mind. Don't get me started on that. I've got to get dressed so I can make it to my nine o'clock. But I do want to hear everything you've been thinking about, Dad. Just don't let the holidays get you this year, okay? Let's do some fun stuff and enjoy ourselves. It's not always good to rehash everything."

"I know. I won't do that."

5

"Okay. Great. I'll see you tomorrow afternoon, maybe five-ish or even six-ish—six-thirty-ish, at very worst."

"Which means seven-ish, at very earliest-ish. I know you."

"You're wrong about me, Father. And you especially don't know David. If I tell him that I promised to be there by six, he'll walk through the door at 5:59, just the way you would. I tell you, you're going to love this man. I'll see you at six."

"Okay. I love you."

"And you are my *idol*. My *icon*. The *symbol* of all that is good in the world."

"Not to mention, the source of your living expenses."

"*Especially* that. Bye."

Ned put down the phone and then looked through the French doors out across the Homestead Resort golf course behind his house. He felt uneasy, and he was trying to think why. It just wasn't like Liz to say, "You're going to *love this man*." She always called the guys she met at college "boys." And what was all the praise about? He was such a "good listener," such a "great guy to talk to." The fact was, *David*—apparently never known as "Dave"—didn't sound like Liz's type. Liz was as smart as her three older brothers, but she had never bothered to let that get in the way of her college life. She was supposedly in her junior year, but she had changed her major almost every semester and had no hope of graduating in four years. *David*, on the other hand, sounded like a stuffed shirt—always studying, knowing *something* about *everything*, and all uptight about punctuality.

*What did I do to deserve this guy?*

Ned opened the door and walked out on the deck. He wondered how much Liz was "hanging out" with this fellow. She had never been capable of keeping a secret; whatever she had on her mind simply spilled out. So why hadn't she mentioned David before? And why had her voice sounded so . . . lilting . . . or whatever it was? The whole thing was worrisome. Liz was *twenty*. It was way too soon for her to find a "boy" she liked, let alone a "man."

Ned's body was cooling now; the air felt cold. But he liked to be outside. All summer, after the golfers cleared the course in the evenings, he had watched as deer trailed off the mountainside and grazed in the grass alongside the fairways. Sometimes, about this time in the morning, he would see a doc and fawn, or several deer, making their way back from Snake Creek, heading toward higher ground for the day. He had seen foxes out on the golf course too, and raccoons got into his hummingbird feeder at night. Lately, big flocks of migrating geese had been flying over in loose, V-shaped formations, honking as they flew, some swooping down to land on a pond in the golf course. He hated to see all that end for the season, but last winter a herd of elk had appeared on the golf course and stayed for a couple of weeks, and the deer were even more abundant then than in summer. He did look forward to that. It was part of why he had chosen to build his house here.

Sometimes, when the sunset was illuminating the clouds over the mountains, or a buck stepped out of the trees, he would catch himself turning, about to call for Kate, to tell her to come and have a look. Then, more than any other time, he felt the return of that fierce level of loneliness that had punished him in the beginning. Mostly, now, he felt only a solemnness that he tried to deny but that lurked just beneath the surface and kept him from enjoying things as fully as he wanted to.

Now, with this new little worry, he indulged himself in a way that he had vowed to stop. He told Kate what he thought. *I don't want Liz to meet anyone. Not yet. She's not ready.*

Kate didn't answer him. Not really. But he always knew what she would say. He heard her voice in his mind.

> *Ned, you worry way too much. Maybe it's time for her to meet someone—while she's still in college.*
>
> *Hey, she'll always be in college. She's going to try every major BYU offers before she finally makes up her mind.*
>
> *That's not fair. She's a pretty good student, really. And I'm glad she has so many interests.*
>
> *Maybe she wants to be like* David. *He knows something about everything.*
>
> *Ned, what am I hearing? I think you're jealous. You're afraid someone else will replace you as her hero.*
>
> *Oh, please. Give me a little credit. The point is, this guy isn't at all right for her.*
>
> *He sounded good to me. He might help Liz settle down a little. Don't make up your mind about him before he even arrives.*

Ned had heard enough. He walked back into the house and on into the bathroom. He pulled off his running clothes, dropped them on the floor, and stepped into the shower. But by the time the water had warmed and was running down his back, he knew what Kate would tell him.

> *Ned, you'll have to let go of that girl sooner or later. You shouldn't depend on her so much.*
>
> *I don't depend on her. I just enjoy having her around. I think you'll have to admit, I do pretty darn well. I cook all right now, and—*
>
> *You defrost. And you nuke. You don't cook.*

*Well, I eat all right. Actually, a lot healthier than when you were doing the cooking.*

*That's because you've turned into a raving fanatic. If you're not running, you're riding your bike.*

*I'm just trying to stay healthy.*

*No. You're making your so-called leisurely life conform to your type-A personality. You don't know how to take life easy.*

But that wasn't fair. Ned was having to make huge adjustments. He had always assumed that Kate would be with him at this stage of his life. She was the one who knew how to curb his compulsive nature. He thought of arguing with her, but he knew he was being weird, carrying on these little dialogues, so he told himself to get on with his day.

He finished his shower, dressed, got himself some granola and yogurt for breakfast, and stepped out onto the deck to eat. He knew it was time to put his outdoor table and chairs away for the winter. If people saw him, they would think he was strange to be out here in the cold, but he was afraid that if any deer crossed the fairway this morning, he might miss seeing them. It was silly to worry about that and he knew it, but it always felt like a gift to see them for a few minutes at the beginning of his day.

*Ned, I know you're trying to ignore me, but we need to talk, whether you want to or not.*

*Talk about what?*

*About you finding someone. You need to get married and you know it.*

*No. I don't. And to tell you the truth, I'm getting a little tired of all the women who keep making overtures.*

9

*They must be desperate people to chase after an old duffer like me, going on sixty.*

*Sixty? You're fifty-three.*

*Well, it's all the same—after fifty, the decades just run together. I wouldn't want a woman who would settle for a guy like me.*

*I'm not going to play that game, Ned. You want me to tell you that you're still good-looking—tall, dark, and handsome, and rich besides. You know that you're a catch.*

*Kate, we just keep saying these same things. Let's let it drop. I don't want to get married. Besides, I've never met a woman I would want to marry—not a single one.*

*What about Sister Schofield?*

*Why do you always bring her up?*

*She's nice. And she's never had a chance to marry.*

*Yes, and she looks like my Great-Aunt Violet.*

*No way. I think she's cute.*

*Cute? Forty-eight-year-old women with frizzy permanents are not cute. They're staring fifty in the face, and they're terrified.*

*Hey, I was almost fifty, and I was cute.*

*No. You were beautiful. And you were smart and funny. And you knew everything about me. So don't blame me if no one looks very good by comparison.*

*Oh, come off it, Ned. I was never a beauty. That was all in your eyes. You've got to quit idealizing me. What about that new woman in the ward? Carol Holly.*

*Her name sounds like a Christmas pun.*

*Well, maybe she was sent to you, just in time for Christmas.*

*The woman is too forward, Kate. I don't mind honesty. But she's blunt.*

*She's pretty.*

*Sort of.*

*Very.*

*In her way. But she's not my type.*

*Neddy, boy, I didn't realize. I think you like her. This is fun.*

*Kate, don't do this. I'm not even slightly interested in her. Just back off on this whole issue. I'm happy the way I am.*

*Don't lie to me, Ned. And especially, don't lie to yourself. If you're not going to show me any more respect than that, I'm not going to talk to you. Whether you know it or not, it's against the rules.*

*That's fine. Don't talk to me. It's something I need to stop.*

*All right. Fine. I agree. I won't nag you anymore. But I sure hate to see what you're doing to yourself.*

"I'm not doing anything to myself," Ned said out loud. And then he told himself, one more time, that he had to stop doing this. He stood up from the table, scanning the golf course and the hills one more time. The mountains weren't as pretty now that most of the leaves were off the trees. In some ways he was looking forward to the snow. The winters were longer and colder here than on the Wasatch Front, but they were like the winters of his childhood. He had grown up in Soda Springs, Idaho, and then had gone to Utah State University, in cold Cache Valley. But after that, he had attended business school at Stanford, and he had ended up spending much of his life in California. During all those years he had been nostalgic about sleigh rides and snowball fights. He was happy for these bonus days now, so warm every afternoon, but he was hoping for three feet of snow before long, in time for Christmas.

As Ned carried his bowl to the kitchen, Kate's words kept clinging to his thoughts. Everyone was telling him the same thing: that he had to find himself a wife. But he couldn't imagine thinking of anyone else the way he had thought of Kate. It wasn't that their marriage had been perfect. Kate had a temper that could flash, and his anger would sometimes rise to a boil. They had gotten in some pretty good fights over the years, and once she had actually begun to pack her clothes, she was so angry. Ned had had to plead with her to stay and talk things out. But in time he had come to feel that only one person had ever gotten so far inside his own skin—and only one ever could. Even after twenty-eight years of marriage, he had sometimes looked across a room at her and been jolted by his love. He had been nuts about her in the beginning, in love with her after one date, but that initial excitement had seemed insignificant compared to the connectedness that had developed between them. They had shared everything for such a long time. How could he even think of starting over with someone else? He just wanted to do his best during the remaining years of his life and then get back to her. *Eternity* had become the word that kept him going.

Kate had died of cancer in August, two years before, at age forty-nine. Since then, he had moved to Utah, mostly to stay close to Liz, who had been starting at BYU that same year. His three sons were married now and scattered, one in Belgium. Liz was the last. She was not much like her mother—except for her sharp tongue—but she always kept the house alive when she was home. That first year, while Ned's new house in Midway was being built, he had lived in a condo in Provo, and Liz had stayed with him. It had helped to have her close while he was adjusting, but she had sometimes made him nervous with all her coming and going, her constant telephone calls, her incessant talk. It was maybe best to have her in smaller doses, but when he did have her around, he swallowed those doses whole, loving to have someone to talk to for a day or two.

He was fine. He really was. And he didn't want to get married. But he knew what lots of people thought—including Liz. And he knew what Kate had told him before she had died. It had been a dismal day for Southern California, rainy. Her suffering had gone on much too long. She had been in the hospital for her surgery soon after she had discovered the lump in her breast, but she had never wanted to go back, and she had fought her way through all the chemotherapy and radiation at home. There had been a couple of months of hope, when the treatments seemed to have worked, but as it turned out, the cancer had spread all through her. All the same, Ned had done plenty of denying, and he had clung to her. On that rainy afternoon she had said to him, "Ned, I can't hold on any longer. I need to go."

But Ned hadn't been ready for that. He had knelt by her bed and taken her in his arms. "Please, don't give up," he had told her. "There are other treatments. We haven't tried everything yet."

But she had cried, softly, her face against his. "I can't do it anymore, Ned," she had told him. "I'm too tired."

Ned had taken some time to accept—the hardest minutes of his life. Finally, he had said, "Okay. You go ahead. I'll follow later."

But that had upset her. "Don't say that, Ned. Your life isn't over. You're going to be around for a long time, and you won't be happy if you're alone. Find someone. It won't bother me. Really, it won't. I need to know you're going to be okay."

He had heard the strain in her voice, the weariness, and he had wanted to comfort her, but still, he told her, "I can't promise that, Kate. Right now, it doesn't even seem possible."

"Okay. I understand. Give it some time. But then you do have to think about it."

"I will."

He had felt the change against his body, her breath coming more deeply. He had lowered her to the bed and slipped his arms out from around her. Her eyes were shut, and she looked more peaceful. She didn't look herself, her face so thin, her color gone, but she was still Kate and she was beautiful, and he wouldn't be himself without her. He knew that, but he let her go. It was three more days before she died, but she never regained consciousness.

Now, Ned walked into the great room and stood before one of the windows. The room was vaulted, with big cathedral windows on both sides and above a fireplace. He and Kate had talked for years about returning to the Mountain West somewhere and building a place like this. He had even built the kitchen she wanted—a big space off the great room with a granite-topped island. He had known as he planned the house that he was making a mistake. After all, he had left his home in California to escape his memories. But this house had existed in his mind so long that it was the only thing he knew to do.

When the doorbell rang, Ned cringed. He had come to know what to expect.

*It's one of them.*

He thought of pretending he wasn't there, but he remembered that the garage door was open and both his cars were in

14

plain sight. Besides, maybe it wasn't what he thought. So Ned walked to the front door and opened it. He knew immediately that he should have followed his first impulse.

"Hi, Ned. How are you this morning?" It was Brenda Schofield—Aunt Violet with too much hair—holding a loaf of bread wrapped in a red-checkered cloth.

"Fine. I was just heading out the door to—"

"Oh, I don't want to take your time. I just thought you'd like to have a nice, warm loaf of bread. I like to bake, but you know, being alone, it seems silly to make just one loaf at a time."

"Well, sure. And you do bake nice things." He saw his chance. "Oh, by the way, I ought to give you back your pie plate while you're here. Just wait a second and I'll get it."

He stuck out his hand like a policeman directing traffic, and the motion, of course, meant, "Stay out there," but the instant he turned, she popped inside. And by the time he got back, she had shut the door. The woman was quick on her feet; he had to give her credit for that. He wondered why she was wearing a dress and dangly earrings at nine in the morning. He had always thought she was sort of pretty—if she wouldn't pile so much makeup on her face—but the only thing he seemed to have in common with her was that they were both mammals who walked upright, on two legs.

"I didn't want to let too much cold air in," she said, her face pinking up as though she knew she had been too bold.

"Well, thanks." He handed her the pie plate and accepted the bread. "Let me just give you this cloth back. I can set it on—"

"Oh, that's fine. Just keep it for now."

All of them knew the same trick. If they left something— a dish or a pan or a bowl—he had to return it. He had started taking things to church with him so he could hand them over there. An immediate return was even better, so he took the bread to his kitchen and then brought back the cloth. But now she had followed him around the corner and was standing in his kitchen.

"Oh, Ned! I've never seen your kitchen. I'd *kill* for a kitchen like this."

"Well, then, I better watch my back."

Brenda had more voice than she really needed, and when it turned into laughter, it shook things.

"One thing I should mention," Ned said. "I'm on a diet, I guess you'd call it. It's all about cutting back on fats and carbohydrates. I don't really eat a lot of bread or baked goods. I love them, and I appreciate what you've brought me, but I'm afraid some of it ends up going to waste."

"Oh, Ned, I'm so sorry. You should have said something sooner." And now she used the arm touch. They all liked that move.

"It's okay. I just thought you ought to know."

"So do you eat a lot of fruit?"

"Yeah. Fruits and vegetables and—"

"Listen, I'll bring you some of my Bing cherries, and some peaches. I love to bottle fruit, but I can't use everything I put up."

"Well, that's nice. But I—"

"Ned, did you grow up in a home where your mother did a lot of canning every fall?"

"Sure. Mom did some of that."

"My mother would spend weeks canning, and I always helped her. To me, when fall comes, it's just an instinct. I grew up in the southern part of the state, and we didn't have such nice fruit as we have up here, so every fall we would—"

"You know, Brenda, I really do have to leave. I have . . . an appointment."

It was a cruel thing to do, but Ned had learned. They operated like salespeople. First they got a foot in the door, then they started a conversation, and before long they were asking you whether you liked to take long walks in the rain. "Sounds wet," Ned had learned to say.

"I'm sorry. I'm such a gabber. I just love to talk with people who—you know—have some depth. Every week during your Sunday School class, I think how much I'd like to ask you some gospel questions. I've done some very deep thinking about— you know—eternal things, but I'm never sure whether I'm on the right track. Maybe sometime we could get together and just—you know—share some thoughts. I'd really love that."

"I'm good at questions, Brenda, but not at answers. I'm the wrong guy to talk to."

"Isn't that interesting you say that." Brenda shook her frizzy brown hair and smiled. "I told a friend of mine the other day that life is all about questions, not answers, and half the joy of life is in the mystery. Don't you think—"

Ned was looking at his watch by then. "Oh, my. I didn't realize what time it was. I'm actually late."

And with that, Brenda finally took her checkered cloth and left. But Ned felt guilty. The woman was nice. And she did mean well. Why had he lied to her? He could have let her talk a little. But he had the frightening feeling that if he ever let her sit down on his couch, she would cling to it. He saw images of ripping fabric as he grabbed her by her ankles and tried to drag her away.

Ned decided he had better get into his car and drive off, just in case she was hiding nearby, checking to see whether he really was going somewhere. But it was a stupid thing to do. He had nowhere to go. He drove to Park City and back—just to kill some time—and by the time he got back, he was depressed. His plan had been to go fly-fishing later that day, since the afternoon temperatures were supposed to be unseasonably warm. Now, he wasn't sure whether he wanted to do that. For one thing, in spite of what Liz had said, he knew he had to clean the house. And yet, he didn't want to do that either—not right now. He wished that he hadn't gone for his run already. He felt a need to do something active, something intense, so he slipped into his padded bicycle pants, then found a dry pair of sweats. His legs were tired, but he wanted to go on a good hard ride. He would work on the house later, before Liz and her boring "friend" arrived.

# Chapter Two

�֎

It was late on Tuesday afternoon when Ned finally sat down to glance through the *Deseret News*. He had put in a busy day, but he had some time now before Liz would be arriving. He had set out to "tidy up" around the house that morning, but one thing had led to another. He really hadn't realized how dirty the place was until he had started cleaning. He loved his house, but it seemed much too large when he cleaned, and the kitchen, with so many countertops, was a terrible collector of mail and other junk that he too often set down intending to take care of later. By the time he finished the house, most of the day was gone, and he hadn't done his daily hour of study for his Gospel Doctrine class. It was after five-thirty by the time he finished; Liz's "five-ish" had come and gone. He wasn't much worried about her vow to be there by six, either. He grabbed the paper, figuring he would have plenty of time to read. As it turned out, however, he had only just begun the sports section when he heard the downstairs security chime. That meant that Liz was coming in through the garage entrance. He looked at his watch. It was 5:59. Ned laughed. She had probably waited a few minutes downstairs, just to get the time exactly right.

Ned heard footsteps on the stairs, and then he saw Liz appear at the door. He loved the way she looked, seemingly thrilled to be home. The girl had a wonderful smile, and he liked the way she was wearing her hair these days—cut short and straight around. She had bright blue eyes that always surprised Ned a little when he hadn't seen her for a while. He had been looking at her for twenty years now, and those eyes still seemed almost unnatural, set off against her nearly black hair. Ned didn't see David, and for a moment he thought she had decided to come home alone after all. He stood to greet Liz, but as she started toward him a tall young man stepped into the room. Ned hugged his daughter and checked out David at the same time. He was the complete preppy: nicely pressed khakis and a blue, oxford-cloth button-down shirt, Polo brand. His brown hair had the look of planned ease, perfectly cut. And drooping over a pair of rich hazel eyes were eyelashes so dark and long they looked false. Ned pulled Liz under his arm and reached out to shake David's hand, and just then the boy released a smile so white that it had to be the work of that bleach stuff dentists were using these days.

*What a pretty boy! I think somebody airbrushed him.*

Ned made up his mind. He didn't like this guy—not at all.

"Dad, this is David Markham," Liz was saying.

"Nice to meet you, sir." *Sir?* And then, of course, the powerful handshake. Ned realized by then that the young man had serious shoulders on him. He was actually *some* specimen. But there was no way Liz could like someone like that. He was all *spectacle.*

"Your house is beautiful, Brother Stevens." *Brother Stevens?* "This view is amazing." He turned—like a pioneer in a bad movie—and gazed west. He even had a strong jaw.

Liz said, "In the summer, Dad and I like to sit out on the

deck after the sun goes behind the mountains. It's always cool up here at night, even in July and August."

David looked at Ned with dog-eyed sincerity, and then, in a heartfelt voice, said, "What a perfect setting this is. You must love it here."

"It's been very comfortable."

Liz walked across the room and flipped the switch that turned on the flame in the fireplace. "How's that for atmosphere?" she asked.

Ned thought it was a little too warm for a fire, but he knew how much Liz liked to have it on, and he loved to see her take pride in the house. She looked as cute as he had ever seen her, dressed in a royal blue blouse and a wraparound denim skirt that showed off her height, her slimness. Her skin was positively glowing. But all that smiling, all that glowing, worried Ned. Maybe her joy wasn't entirely about arriving home.

"Sit down. Please. I made a dinner reservation for seven o'clock over at the Snake Creek Grill. But it only takes about ten minutes to get there." He looked at his watch. "We have forty-five minutes before we have to leave."

"Dad's always on time," Liz said. Then she smiled at Ned. "And what about us? I told you six, and we're here at six."

"Actually, by my watch, it was 5:59," Ned admitted.

"Oh, good," David said. "I have my watch set about five minutes early all the time, just so I won't be late for anything. I thought we were a couple minutes late."

*Oh, brother.* Ned liked to be on time, but he wasn't quite that nervous about it.

The fireplace area in the great room was set off by two hefty tan couches and two big rust-colored chairs. Ned sat down on the couch across from the fire and motioned for them to take the chairs. Some instinct told him that was the arrangement he preferred.

David walked toward one of the chairs, but then he stopped and looked out the window. "Look at the way the sunset is making those clouds glow," he said.

Ned liked that. It was something he often watched himself. But then he noticed David's perfectly shined loafers. Who shined loafers with that kind of care? The guy was vain.

"So, David, Liz tells me you're from Connecticut. What part? I know some people from Darien."

"That's close. We live in Greenwich."

"Maybe you know the Mitchells. They're LDS. Probably in your stake."

"I knew a Melissa Mitchell. I think she was from there."

"You didn't know her parents?"

"No, I don't think so." David was still gazing out the window.

"David went on a mission to Scotland," Liz said. "He's a senior now. He'll graduate in April."

Ned didn't like that. He knew what happened to these RMs once they hit their senior year. The last thing they wanted was to leave BYU without a wife. "What are you majoring in, David?" Ned asked.

"I have a double major in history and philosophy."

*Oh, great. Just try to find a job with a degree like that.*

"He's planning to go to medical school, Dad. He's got a lot of applications out. He'll be doing his interviews before long."

*How many guys claim they're going to med school? I'll believe that when he shows me a letter of acceptance.* "Is that right? What field of medicine are you interested in?"

"I'm thinking I'd like to be a pediatrician."

*Wait until some kid pukes on those pretty shoes.*

"He's applying to all the best schools. Harvard. Yale. Johns Hopkins."

"I've never been to Midway before," David said. "I didn't know it was so beautiful. How did the town get its name?"

"I think it was actually midway between two forts, or something like that, but people from here have a standard answer to that question. They always say it's 'midway to heaven.'"

"I think they're right, too. So how long have you lived here?"

"Just over a year."

Liz laughed, for no apparent reason, and then said, "You ought to follow Dad through one of his days, David. He gets up before it's even daylight, and he runs up Snake Creek Canyon, and then he's got things going on all day. He golfs three or four times a week, and he goes on long bicycle rides. In the summer he fly-fishes, and in the winter he skis—cross-country on the golf courses, or downhill over at Deer Valley. And in between he's always on some reading project—trying to find out everything there is to know about the Civil War or Book of Mormon archeology or whatever he's into at the moment."

"Wow. That sounds great."

Liz was making those seal-barking noises again. "It is. Except that he's a fanatic. He supposedly came up here to live the simple life, but he's managed to put himself on this madman's schedule. He wears himself out playing all day."

David smiled with all those big white teeth. He nodded toward Ned. "But look what great shape he's in. If you ask me, he's got life figured out."

*The kid is slick. Soooooo slick. Liz tries to make me sound like*

23

*some kind of combination lunatic and lazy bum, but he's smart enough to act like he admires me.*

"I wish my dad would learn to enjoy himself a little, just once in a while."

"What does your dad do, David?"

"That's hard to say. He's got his fingers into all kinds of things. Too many."

*What's that supposed to mean? Is he an entrepreneur or a burglar? This kid is evasive.* "Tell me a little about yourself, David. What do you enjoy doing?"

"Everything. That's my problem. I'm a jack-of-all-trades and master of none."

"That's not true," Liz said. "He doesn't like to brag. His problem is, he does so many things well, he doesn't know which ones to emphasize."

David smiled again, but this time with lots of humility. "She exaggerates," he said, "but you probably know that."

"No, Dad, really. He was a sports star in high school, and he was on the newspaper staff and in the choir and . . . a lot of other stuff."

David shook his head. "Liz talked to my sister, who's even more of an exaggerator than Liz is. I did play lots of sports, but I wasn't that great at any of them. And the thing is, Brother Stevens, I just—"

"Why don't you just call me Ned?"

"Well . . . okay. But anyway, my dad and I talked it over a long time ago. Unless you're a super athlete, and you're hoping for a career in the pros, sports can take way too much of your time. I decided that my future would be in medicine, or at least in something that would require a good education. So I've tried to give most of my attention to my studies."

"And he does, too. He's a real brain, Dad."

*How do you know, Liz? Did he tell you so?*

But David was rolling his eyes. "You know what I'd like to learn?" he said. "Fly-fishing. Do you think next summer, before I head off to med school, you could teach me the basics?"

*I'll help you head off to med school. That's what I'll do.* "Sure. I'd be happy to. Have you done much fishing?"

"Not really. I've done some deep-sea fishing with my family—but only a couple of times, when we were on vacation. I don't know the first thing about fishing in a stream."

"If you can go off deep-sea fishing on vacation, it sounds like your father has done very well for himself."

"I guess you'd say that. Do you fish mostly in the Provo River?"

*What's wrong with this kid? He won't give a straight answer.* "I fish the Provo some, but an awful lot of people fish it. I like some of the little streams around here better."

"Liz tells me that you had a business in California that you sold out. What kind of business was it?"

"I got into consulting when it was still the new thing. I did leadership seminars, and then I branched out into doing various kinds of management workshops. I traveled a lot in the beginning, but eventually I had a good-sized team of people working for me. It was a good living, but I got tired of it. I pushed too hard, too long. Besides, I got such a good offer to sell out, it seemed pointless to stay at it any longer."

What Ned didn't say was that he had lost the heart to go on after Kate had died. The work had lost its meaning, and he had already accumulated more money than he would ever need. Kate had grown up in Logan, and for years she and Ned had talked about moving back to Utah and building a house in the mountains. They had even talked about Heber Valley. Ned had felt at times as though he had put his life on automatic pilot and simply carried out the plan for lack of any other idea about what he ought to do. But he also liked to think that he was doing what Kate had wanted, and that maybe she was able to stay close enough to him to share some of their dream. Sometimes when he awoke at night, he seemed to feel her there, sleeping next to him, even believed for a moment that he heard her breathing, softly, the way she had for all those years. The pain was always sharp again when he realized he was alone.

Ned and David talked about Ned's life, about his sons and six grandchildren, and then Ned made a couple more stabs at finding out more about David and his family. Liz kept claiming that David was lovely and talented, but David remained unwilling to say anything specific about himself. That worried Ned. What was he ashamed of? And Liz's enthusiasm was even more of a worry. She was all flushed with excitement. She kept looking over at David, and the two would exchange glances that were clearly those little intimate understandings that could come only from time spent together. There was no way that these two were merely *buddies*. They must have been dating all fall.

Ned finally told Liz and David that it was time to start thinking about heading over to the restaurant. David had left his things downstairs, it turned out, and Ned had to wonder what that meant. Was Liz toying with the idea of putting him in one of the downstairs bedrooms, by hers? But David seemed to understand that he was staying in the loft, two floors away from Liz. He carried his suitcase—*and a hang-up bag!*—upstairs, and then came down talking about the beautiful view of the valley from the balcony in the loft. The guy was a scenery freak. Or at least he claimed to be. It was hard to trust a young guy who made that much fuss about mountains and sunsets. Ned thought the scenery that *actually* held his interest was about five-foot-nine, willowy, and, at the moment, way too perky.

The dinner at the Snake Creek Grill was excellent, as always, and David was enthusiastic about that, too, but he still wouldn't come clean about himself. Liz ended up doing most of the talking, either praising David or telling stories about school and roommates and the test she had taken that afternoon—the one that was "outrageously unfair." At one point she talked about Kate, and about the long, destructive course of the cancer that had taken her life. "I was the only one home with Dad by then," she said. "We could see what was happening to her, but we didn't want to accept it. Especially me. I was a teenager and I needed a mom. She tried so hard, but by the end, she just couldn't concentrate—because of the medicine—and she slept most of the time. But Dad and I talked about *everything*. Even all my boyfriend problems. He got me through." She reached over and took hold of Ned's hand.

"We got each other through," Ned told her.

Ned didn't like to think about those times, but he did cherish the closeness he had felt to Liz and the amazing maturity she had shown. He thought of the night Liz had brought her prom date to the house. Kate had been in the midst of chemotherapy then, but she had wanted to see Liz with her date, and wanted Ned to take pictures. Kate had been terribly nauseated that night and could barely hold her head up. Liz had sensed what was happening and had warned Ned. The two had helped Kate back to her bedroom, and then Liz had knelt in her long, silver dress and held a basin as her mother vomited. Ned had taken over, told Liz to go ahead, but Liz had sat next to Kate and stroked her hair until she had fallen asleep.

Ned looked down at the table, took some long breaths. When he finally glanced up, he saw that tears had come into David's eyes. It crossed Ned's mind that maybe David wasn't such a bad guy—but then, who couldn't work up a little emotion about a young woman losing her mom?

After the crème brûlée—which David did gush over—and the short drive back home, Liz wanted to watch Jane Austen's *Emma*, which David had never seen. Ned had watched it with Liz twice—once more than he had wanted to—and he didn't really want to sit through it again. He decided to finish reading the newspaper, upstairs, while Liz and David watched on the big-screen TV in the basement, but after a while he started to worry about what might be going on down there. He knew it was a sneaky thing to do, but he walked quietly down the stairs, hoping to turn the corner from the stairway before they slipped away from each other.

When he reached the last step, he waited and looked into the dark room. Over the top of the couch back, he saw two heads, too close. The couch was a double recliner, but they had scrunched together on the same end, and they were lying back. He thought about shouting, "I caught you!" but he couldn't tell for sure what was going on. David didn't seem to have his arm around Liz. Ned cleared his throat, to announce his presence, and then walked around the back of the couch and sat on another recliner, but they didn't have enough shame to separate themselves, and Ned saw *exactly* what he suspected: David was holding her hand!

*Just friends, huh? Buddies. Do you think I'm stupid enough to believe that?*

Ned was no longer worried. He was scared. He needed to find out who this kid was and what he was up to, and he needed to do it immediately. He thought of his friend Harold Mitchell. It was after eleven in Connecticut, but old Harold never had been one to go to bed early. "I don't think I want to watch this again," Ned told Liz, and he walked upstairs. He had chosen his words carefully. He wanted them to think he wasn't coming back. That would leave him room for one more chance to pop in and see what kind of moves ol' David might have. As he walked up the stairs, a little scene developed in his mind. After Harold gave him the real goods on David and his family, maybe Ned would return to announce, "I don't want *your kind* in my house. Grab your *hang-up bag,* scenery-boy, and make tracks out of this valley."

Ned thought he had Harold's number in his Palm Pilot, but he didn't, so he had to dig up his old Rolodex, and by then, he was a little worried about the time getting on toward 11:30 in the East, on a Tuesday night. He called all the same, and after four rings, a rather groggy voice said, "Yeah?"

Ned didn't care. He had to do this. "Harold?"

"Yes. Who's this?"

"Ned Stevens, out in Utah. I know how late it is out there, and I'm sorry, but I've got a bit of an emergency going on here."

There was not a sound on the other end of the line. Harold didn't seem to be all that happy about the call.

"Do you know an LDS family in your area by the name of Markham?" Ned forged on. "They live in Greenwich."

"Are you talking about Gilbert Markham?"

"I'm not sure. They have a son named David."

"Yes. I know the family. Very well. Elder Markham was our stake president until not too long ago. Now he's the Area Authority Seventy."

"Oh."

Ned could almost hear the impatience in the silence that followed, and then he heard it resoundingly in the question. "What's the emergency, Ned?"

"Well . . . my daughter has been dating David. He's out here at BYU. I'm just not too sure about the guy."

"Ned, if you think this is funny, you're wrong."

"No, no. He seems like one of these *slick* kids who pretends to be pure as the driven snow, and then turns out to be . . . you know . . . immoral, and everything else. I've already seen some indication of that."

"Ned, my daughter would give anything in the world to get a date with that boy. I think every girl in this part of the country is in love with him. He was a *superstar* athlete—the best high school athlete I've ever seen. I saw that kid play offense and defense in the state football finals and win the game almost single-handedly. He's not just skilled, he's got heart. And he's a tremendous leader."

"Well, yeah. I got the idea he was a good athlete, but—"

"Ned, sports are a sideline to this young man. He represented the state of Connecticut at Boys' Nation. He gave the valedictorian speech at his high school, and it was so well done that the AP picked it up and printed a big section of it in all the newspapers around here. I saw it in the *New York Times*. I also heard him give a talk at seminary graduation, and I told my wife, 'This boy will be an apostle someday—if he's not the president of the United States.'"

"Republican or Democrat?"

"What?"

"Well, he seems a little too slippery to me—like some of those con artists in Congress. He's so—"

"Ned, wait a minute. You got me out of bed because you're

worried about your daughter dating David Markham? Is that what you're telling me?"

"Well . . . yes. I just felt like I needed to know for sure what kind of—"

"Ned, you should pay a *dowry* to get that boy—all the cows in Utah, barns included. If I thought I could win him for my daughter, I'd fight you in a duel."

"Okay. Well, I appreciate . . . you know . . . your opinion."

"Ned, are you okay? Ever since Kate passed away, I've had the feeling you're not quite yourself."

"No, no. I'm fine. It's just that I caught David with my daughter downstairs, and he was—you know—trying to put some moves on her."

"What are you talking about? That doesn't sound like the boy I know."

"Well, it wasn't too serious . . . yet. But he was already holding her hand and he had only been down there with her a few minutes."

"He was *holding her hand*? That's what you're worried about?"

"Not exactly. I just . . . noticed some things."

"Ned, have you talked to anyone about the grieving process? Have you seen any sort of professional?"

"Hey, it's nothing like that. I'm fine. But I do worry about my daughter. I'm not willing to throw her at anyone, just because he *looks good* on the outside. That superficial stuff doesn't mean a thing to me. I'm sorry I bothered you. Go back to bed." Ned pressed the "off" button on his phone.

*Harold always has been too impressed by titles. So David's father is an Area Authority? That doesn't prove anything.*

Ned sat back and tried to think. Gradually his embarrassment

31

began to settle in. He never should have told Harold about the hand holding. That did sound pretty innocent, stated as an isolated fact. But Harold hadn't seen all the other clues.

Or . . . maybe . . . Ned had been just a little hasty in his judgment.

Yet, the more he thought about it, the more he was able to identify a pattern of behavior that had set off all the alarms he had been hearing.

*Kate, this situation doesn't look good to me.*

*I thought we weren't going to talk anymore.*

*We're not. I just need to run this one thing by you. I feel like our daughter is in danger of messing up her life. This David guy is not like her. She's open and straightforward. She doesn't hide things.*

*For crying out loud, Ned, would you like him better if he bragged all the time? I'm impressed that he didn't make a big deal out of himself.*

*But see, that's just the point. That's what he wants us to think—that he's sweet and humble. He knows that I'll find out all that stuff about his dad and his achievements, sooner or later. He probably knew darn well that I would talk to Harold. I'll tell you what I see. I'm discovering a young man who's calculating. He knows how to impress people. He's got everybody bamboozled.*

*Ned, I do believe you're losing your mind.*

*No. Think about it. I've always said, if something looks too good to be true, it probably is. I say "buyer beware" on this boy. He's the sort of guy who gets good grades and goes to church and seems to do everything right, and one day you discover a ski mask under his bed and find out he's been sticking up convenience stores.*

*Right. All you have to do is look at those big, beautiful eyes of his, and you know he's a hold-up man.*

*Now you're talking like a woman. You like him because he's cute.*

*He is cute. I'll admit that. Now you admit that you're jealous of him.*

*Jealous? Oh, right. I'm jealous of a sweet, young boy who thinks he can call me "brother" and I won't see right through him. Harold Mitchell is a nice guy, but he's never been very perceptive. He doesn't delve beneath the surface of things.*

*And you do?*

*Yes, as a matter of fact. I see plenty. For one thing, I think it's very interesting that Liz has never lied to me, and now she's started. I don't think that's just a coincidence. I think it has everything to do with that boy.*

*What did she lie about?*

*She never once mentioned David, even though I always ask her about what she's been doing and who she's been going out with. And then, when she finally mentions him, what does she say? He's her friend. Well, you tell me. Are they acting like friends?*

*Ned, you monitor her too much. She wouldn't dare tell you if she did like a guy. You're always telling her not to get married.*

*That's because she isn't ready to get married. She's only twenty.*

*But Ned, you have to let her grow up her own way. She's got to make her own decisions.*

*Not when I see disaster ahead. I can't let that happen.*

*I'm going to walk quietly downstairs right now and find out what's going on.*

*Ned, no. What if your dad had sneaked into the living room when we were—*

*That was different. And you ought to know that. I'm sorry I even bothered you.*

Ned got up and walked carefully from his office across the tiled area between the kitchen and the great room. He slowed near the entrance to the stairway. He knew a place—*beneath the surface*—that made a little thump if you stepped on it too hard. He paused there, then quietly walked down the steps. As he turned the corner, he stared into the darkened room. At first he thought they had disappeared, but then he saw that their two heads were together, *touching,* barely showing above the couch back. He had them. He took one more step, felt along the wall for the light switch, and then suddenly threw on the light.

Nothing happened. Their heads didn't move. And then Liz said, "Dad, turn the light off. It's hard to see the screen."

*Are you my daughter? When did you become so brazen?*

Ned stepped around the couch, so the two had to face him. Sure enough, Liz was leaning against David, her head on his shoulder. She raised up a little now. "Why don't you sit down and watch this with us, Dad?" she asked. "It's *so* good."

"All right. I just might *do* that!"

"What?"

She didn't get it. She was acting as though nothing were going on. And there was David, looking perfectly innocent, sort of half smiling.

"Really, Brother Stevens, you ought to watch with us," David said. "I just love these Jane Austen stories. A lot of guys call them chick flicks, but I think they miss the irony in the social satire."

*Oh, brother.*

Ned sat down. He knew for sure now: These two were more than friends—*much more.* He didn't like this movie, but he was not going to leave until his daughter was safe.

But then Liz showed the kind of audaciousness she was learning from this guy. She got up and walked to the wall by the stairway and she turned the light back off. And then, when she sat down—or rather, *lay down*—in the recliner, she snuggled up next to him once again. In front of her own father!

Ned stayed. After half an hour of watching the movie, he was fighting sleep, but still he stayed, and he kept his eyes open as best he could. But somewhere in the never-ending ending of this tedious movie, he must have slipped off to sleep. He was awakened suddenly by his daughter saying, "Dad, it's over. David and I are going to bed."

*"What?"* He sat up straight, popping the recliner upright in the process.

"You fell asleep, Dad. But it's time to go to bed."

By then Ned had spotted David, across the room, about to climb the stairs. He was apparently heading for the loft, as planned. Ned took a breath, tried to get his heart to stop pounding. "See you in the morning, Brother Stevens," David said, and he smiled with that mouthful of white teeth.

"Yeah. Good night," Ned mumbled. But he knew he had to do something. It was exactly that kind of stuff—that smile, those sweet words—that told Ned he was right about this guy.

# Chapter Three

Ned thought he wouldn't get up quite so early the next morning—since he had stayed up later than usual. But by six o'clock he was wide awake, and by six-thirty he was worrying so much about David that he decided he would go for his run, even though the sun wasn't up yet. He pulled on his gear and tiptoed through the house. He didn't want to wake Liz or David, and actually, he didn't even want Liz to know he was out running so early. She would have something to say again about him being a fanatic.

He turned off the security system, and then he slipped out the front door and down the front stairs. He did a few stretches before he poked the button on his sports watch and jogged up the street. He headed up the road past the Wasatch golf course and into Snake Creek Canyon. It didn't take him long to realize that his legs were still hammered from all the running and bike riding he'd done the last few days. He told himself to take things easy, not worry about exceeding the new high point he had reached, and just get in a nice little run. But when he got past the power plant and started up the first serious hill, he realized he would have to give up much sooner than usual and do most of his running in the relatively flat part of the valley. Still, he got through that first hard climb, caught his breath a little on an easier section of the road, and then dug in to make it up one more steep hill. He was running slowly with his head down, breathing harder than usual, when he heard something up ahead. For a moment, he thought that a deer must be running across the road, but what he made out, up the road, was a dark human figure running toward him.

Quite a few people walked or ran this canyon, but most of them, not so early. Still, Ned didn't pay much attention. He was preoccupied, digging down for what strength was left in him. The one thing he was sure of was that he would let this guy go by before he gave up on the hill and turned around. As the runner neared, Ned glanced up to say hello. But then he heard, "Brother Stevens, is that you?"

The truth refused to register in Ned's head for a moment, even though he knew very well what he was seeing—hearing. "David?"

"Yeah." He slowed, but just as Ned was about to stop, the boy swung around and started uphill, joining him. "Wow. This is a tough run. I don't know how you do it every day."

"How far up did you go? All the way to the top?"

"Oh, no. I just ran to the end of the pavement. I didn't want to run on the dirt road in the dark."

Ned couldn't believe it. The end of the pavement was what Ned considered the top. That had been his goal for a year, someday to make it to that point, but he had never come close—except in his car. And now David was running just a little ahead, pushing Ned faster than he wanted to go. Ned was trying desperately to pant, not gasp, but he drew in enough air to say, as casually as he could, "What are you doing up so early?"

"I don't know. It's just habit. I run most mornings, and I have to get up pretty early if I'm going to read the scriptures before I head off to school. I was going to be lazy this morning, but I don't know . . . I woke up, so I thought I might as well try this run you mentioned last night. Boy, though, I had no idea it was going to be so hard." He sounded as though he had just picked up a baby and was saying, "She's a heavy little thing, isn't she?" He wasn't even breathing—at least not so Ned could hear him.

"I'm having a hard time this morning," Ned said. "I've spent too much time on my bike lately, along with my running."

"Wow, you're a better man than I am. I gotta tell you, I can't make it back up to the top. I think I'll just peel off pretty soon and head back down."

Ned was running much too hard now, letting David force him faster and faster. His lungs were scorching, his legs losing power. "Well, let's just head back together," he said in a burst. He saved up some breath for a few more strides, and then added, "This'll be enough for me today."

"Oh, no. Don't let me ruin your run. It's still early. I'll go back and maybe help Liz get some breakfast started."

There were so many things wrong with that statement. First off, Liz wouldn't be up for *hours*. And more important, Ned didn't want David going into her bedroom to wake her. But the crucial matter was more pressing: If Ned kept up this pace for twenty more yards, he would collapse. So he decided not to discuss the issue. He merely stopped.

David's momentum carried him ahead for a few paces before he stopped and looked back. Ned wanted desperately to start making excuses, but he couldn't have done it without wheezing, so he merely waited until David returned, and then he managed to get out, "Hey, it's your vacation."

"Well, thanks, Brother . . . or Ned. It's nice of you to go easy on me."

Ned was sure that David knew what was really going on. The guy was playing him again—actually putting him down while he was faking all this admiration. But it wasn't working. *How dumb do you think I am, Mr. Slick?*

Ned started walking, taking long, smooth breaths and trying not to make any noise. But David began to jog again, and Ned felt he had to keep up. He was just glad they were heading downhill now.

"Ned, you teach Gospel Doctrine, right?"

"Yes, I do."

"I wish I was more of a gospel scholar. I read the scriptures, but I don't read much background stuff. There's just a lot I don't understand. When I listen to some of the religion professors at the Y, I think maybe that's what I ought to do—get a job where I'm expected to study the gospel all the time."

The truth was, Ned thought some of those BYU professors made the gospel too complicated. He didn't want to think about theology all day; he wanted to live a good life. But what came out of Ned, in a burst of breath, was, "Do you want to take a vow of poverty?"

David laughed. "That's what my dad says. But I think about a lot of things, and it would be fun to dig into some really meaty topics with the students. Like, for instance, have you ever thought much about humility?"

*No, but you should.* "What do you mean?"

"Well, I just think it's interesting to ask, what's it good for? Everybody always tells you that you've got to have a dream— you know, that you've got to accomplish something really big. But the harder you work to improve yourself or do well in your career, the more attention you get, or the richer you get, and it seems like it's harder than ever to be humble. So I started thinking, what's more important, to achieve or to be humble? And when I tried to think why humility is so important, I couldn't think why God cared quite so much about it. And yet, Christ keeps saying he comes to the poor and the meek and those that suffer. So how come we all run around trying to make money and become powerful and famous? It just seems like most of our efforts are self-defeating. A guy is better off to be poor, or have leprosy or a palsy, or something like that."

At the moment, Ned was the one with a palsy. He was about to die. Even downhill, if he kept running this hard, he was soon going to need an ambulance. He had to do something, and suddenly he knew what it was. "Aaahhh," he yelped, pulling up.

David stopped and turned back. "What happened? Are you all right?"

"Hamstring," Ned muttered. He bent over and drew in all the air he could.

"Oh, no. I've had those. It hurts like crazy, doesn't it? You better keep walking or it'll really tie up on you."

"Yeah." Still, Ned held his ground. He needed a couple more minutes. But he was starting to recognize his problem. Was he going to fake a limp all the way home now—or all weekend? It was true what people said—one lie does lead to another. So Ned kept breathing, and he rubbed hard on his right hammy, and then he said, "It just sort of grabbed there for a minute. I think it's all right. Let's walk for a few minutes, and then maybe I can manage a slow jog the rest of the way in."

"If you want, I can run down and get my car and come back for you."

That was tempting, just to send him down the canyon, but

Ned didn't want to overplay the thing and get Liz all upset. "No, no." He started to walk. "It's not bad at all."

"I hope I wasn't running too fast. I get talking and I forget—"

"Oh, no. Not at all. I've been taking it easy this morning. That's probably what messed me up—changing my stride." The first lie had been an act of desperation. Ned didn't feel all that bad about that one. But this new one was an act of vanity, and now he felt some shame. Maybe he did need to think more about humility.

The two walked, and Ned didn't limp. He needed to repent, and a fake limp wasn't a very good start.

"So what do you think, though? What's so good about humility?"

*You don't let up, do you?*

It was something Ned actually had thought about. But he didn't believe the subject was all that complicated. "It's the basis for everything in the gospel," he said. "If you glorify yourself, you can't learn. You don't even see where you need to improve. And if you're self-centered, you don't see the needs of others."

"Right. And that's why we're supposed to forget ourselves. But we don't forget ourselves. Especially young people. We're all wrapped in our careers and our dreams for the future, and so everything is about us."

"Maybe so. But you have to get yourself ready for life—and get an education so you can provide for your family."

"I know. That's what I keep thinking. But if humility is the most important thing, maybe our careers shouldn't matter quite so much."

"David, you can't try to be poor because you think that will help you be humble. Think about the parable of the talents.

You're supposed to do something with what you've got. The important thing is to do things that are worthwhile and not become impressed with yourself. That's the challenge."

"Okay. Right. That's good. That's one of the things I've been thinking. But here's something else I've had spinning around in my mind. God is all powerful, but he's also all good. Or in other words, he's perfect in humility. If God were all powerful, but not humble, he would be dangerous—more dangerous than Satan."

"That's interesting."

"Yeah, it is. And I think it tells us why we have to learn humility ourselves. If we're ever going to make any progress in being more like the Lord, we have to gain greater powers—develop all our capacities—and yet, not let those powers make us proud."

Ned was still a little preoccupied by his near-death experience, and he was only slowly getting his wind back, but this last idea struck home. "That's a very interesting thought, David."

"I can't take all the credit for it. One of my religion professors told us something kind of like that. I'm just giving the idea my own twist."

Ned glanced toward David, who looked back at Ned. The thought crossed Ned's mind that this kid wasn't all show. He had done some thinking. But talk, no matter how well dressed up, was still cheap. Ned had learned in life, it was almost always better to trust his first instincts.

"You know what bothers me, Ned? I can't seem to do both. I improve myself a little at times, but when I do, I'm really prideful. And pride is a hard thing to fight. You can talk to yourself about it, but it seems to come whether you want it or not.

The only thing that seems to get rid of it is to have something bad happen. When I need the Lord, that's when I get humble."

"I know all about that, of course. We all have that struggle."

"Losing your wife must have been about as big a test as a man can face."

Ned couldn't believe that David would come out with something like that. The guy had no right to start digging into Ned's personal life. So Ned tried to say something neutral. "I'm handling it okay. I know I'll see her again."

"But I can imagine how hard it must be. I guess you can tell, I have some very strong feelings toward your daughter. When I think about her leaving mortality before I do, it already scares me."

"David, she's twenty years old."

"I know. That's not what I'm saying. I know she's not likely to die soon. I just mean that it's hard for me to be away from her very long, and we've only known each other a few weeks."

Now Ned was angry. This was exactly what he had been afraid of all along. This kid was getting serious—really serious. He'd be waving a diamond under Liz's nose any day now. But Ned wasn't going to let that happen. Liz needed some years to come into her own, and David was all wrong for her. He was *too* religious—too *BYU*. He couldn't even go for a run without starting a doctrinal discussion. Liz wasn't like that. She didn't advertise her religion—she lived it. She was as naturally faithful as anyone Ned knew. If she married David, he would have her confessing her sins while she was out for a jog.

"I can run now," Ned said. He took off a little fast, however, and he regretted it when David kept up the same pace all the way home. And back at the house, Ned got a terrible fright. When he walked up the stairs from the basement, he found himself looking straight at Liz. It wasn't Liz herself that scared him. It was the realization that the sun was barely up and she was already showered and dressed and looking brighter than a sunbeam. Something strange was going on. "What are you doing up?" Ned asked.

"I woke up and I felt so great, I decided I wanted to get an early start on the day. I decided to cook you two something good for breakfast, but I thought you were both still in bed. I should have known better."

This was not good. This was a possible sign of some deep-rooted personality disorder. No one could change that much, that suddenly. Liz had never once, in her entire life, gotten up early on her own—at least not without some serious reason—and when she *had* gotten up, she had never once talked about "getting an early start on the day." David was stealing the "self" right out of the girl, and although some might consider the change an improvement, all Ned could think was that he wanted his daughter back.

"Your dad's an animal," David said. "I ran that mountain he runs every morning, and it almost killed me off. Then he pulls up with a hammy on the way down, and he walks a little bit, shakes it off, and runs on home."

"I know. I told you that's how he is."

*Okay, Kate. Here's what I'm talking about. The guy was up there not fifteen minutes ago, talking about rising to perfection and needing just a little more humility to go with his greatness, and now he's already down here spreading manure. He heard me breathing like a dragon. He knows very well that he's in better shape than I am, but he's trying to make me look good in front of Liz—just so I'll like him. How stupid does he think I am?*

44

*Not half as stupid as I think you are. The boy had some great things to say up there. He's just the kind of young man I want for Liz. He'll have her thinking about things that really matter—and she hasn't always done that.*

*I'll bet he doesn't talk to her about humility. He whispers in her ear—like Satan. And slips his arm around her. Don't tell me he hasn't kissed her yet.*

*Well, I would hope so. You kissed me on our second date.*

*Oh, that little peck? That wasn't a kiss. It was just a—*

"Dad?"

"Oh. What?"

"I asked you twice—what do you want for breakfast?"

"I'm sorry. I thought you were talking to David."

Liz was leaning against the refrigerator, her shoulder against the cherry-wood-paneled front—and she was smiling. There was a serious chance that the girl was actually a clone—or some kind of alien who had the power to take on the appearance of an earthling. She and tooth-boy were actually here to burglarize his home. "But what do you want for breakfast?" she was asking.

"Has anyone seen Liz Stevens? She's my daughter. I thought she was coming home for the weekend, but I haven't seen her."

"Shush. You're not funny."

Ned wiped his sweaty forehead with his sleeve. "Liz, you've never heard of breakfast. I've been trying to get you to eat a meal in the morning since you were ten years old."

"Oh, Dad, you know so little about me." She used her teasing smile, the one she had been using to get what she wanted from him all her life. "You don't realize how much I've grown up lately. After all, breakfast is the most important meal of the day."

*Right.*

45

Ned decided he wasn't going to joke anymore about this. There was actually nothing funny about what was going on here. Mind control was an ugly thing. Early-bird boy was a lot more dangerous than he looked. "I still eat my granola and low-fat yogurt," Ned said. "I don't fry things, and I don't eat sugary cereals."

Liz looked at David, who had walked over to the kitchen window. He was staring, apparently watching what was left of the sunrise. "Do you want the same thing?" she asked.

"Is it homemade granola or that commercial kind?"

"It's all natural," Ned said. His voice betrayed a bit more pride than he was proud of. He walked to the cabinet and pulled out the box, then showed it to David.

"Oh, that stuff is bad. They put all kinds of junk in it to sweeten it up and make it stick together. It's 18 percent saturated fat. I'll just have some fruit, if you have any, and maybe some whole-wheat toast. No butter."

*All right, Kate. That seals it. This boy talks like a Christian, but he sets up ambushes. He finds tricky little ways to put me down every time he gets a chance.*

*You know, Ned, I've read that that commercial granola is not that good for you. He's got a point.*

Ned was looking at the box, searching desperately for proof that David was wrong. But there it was: 18 percent. And Ned had been gobbling it up every day for at least a year.

"I know you think you're a health nut, Dad, but David is in a league of his own. That's why I'm so amazed that you could keep up with him when he's running. Did you know that he enters those iron-man races?"

"Liz, you're exaggerating again. I ran in *one*. And that was

46

just because after my mission I wanted to do something to get myself back into condition."

"But you almost won the thing."

"I did not. Who told you that? My sister?"

"Your mother, I think."

David turned from looking out the window and leaned back against the cabinets. He stared at the floor, looking embarrassed. "Well, it's not true. I didn't 'almost win.'"

"What place did you come in?"

"I don't remember."

"Yes, you do. I think it was second."

"No, it wasn't."

"Third."

"No, really. It was like fourth or fifth—or worse. And not that many people run in those things."

"Well, I'm glad it turned out that way," Ned said. He waited for David to look up at him. "If you'd won, you might have been in danger of losing your humility."

It was a good jab, and Ned enjoyed it. But he saw a hurt look come over David's face, as though he had just been gouged.

*Ned, that wasn't nice.*

But Ned knew that already.

Ned ate his granola, no matter what David thought of the stuff, and afterward, he told Liz and David he wanted to go shopping for groceries for Thanksgiving dinner. "Why don't you two ride over to Heber City with me?" he said. "You can help me decide what we need."

The truth was, Ned was feeling guilty about his nasty little comment about David's humility, and he was trying to be a little more friendly.

"I think I'll let you and Liz go ahead," David said. "I need to spend part of the day studying. If we're going to play golf later on, I should get in some book time this morning."

"Oh, come on, David," Liz said. "Go with us. You can study when we get back."

Actually, Ned had liked David's idea. He wanted a few minutes with his daughter. If he could point out just a few of the inconsistencies he had noticed about David—in a subtle, kindly way, of course—maybe she would start to see through him.

But when David showed little interest in grocery shopping, Liz began to waver. "Maybe I should stay and start on my paper. Dad, you probably know what you want, don't you?"

But this was another matter. Ned wasn't about to leave these two in his house alone for an hour. "Ah, come on. I don't know what David likes. Maybe we can drive past Soldier Hollow too." He looked at David. "That's where the Nordic ski events for the Olympics were held. It's worth having a look at."

And so the two gave in, but only after vows that they would study when they got back—and play only nine holes later on. Ned couldn't believe all this. Liz had never let school ruin any of her holidays, ever.

The three took the drive in Ned's big Land Rover, and all went pretty well, except for David's smart-aleck question about the gas mileage Ned got. This was clearly a little attack on Ned for wasting fossil fuels, but Ned had the answer. "It does use a lot of gas, but I figure the cost of the thing probably kept several families eating for a year. We all have to do our bit to stimulate the economy, you know."

David only laughed. And then he admitted a fault. "I'm

afraid I have a weakness when it comes to cars myself," he said. "I get that from my dad."

"That wasn't much of a car you parked out in front of my house," Ned said.

David and Liz both laughed. "That's my sweet little Corolla," David said. "She'll soon be an adult. She's approaching twenty-one."

"Maybe you get your *taste* in cars from your dad, but apparently not the cars themselves."

David laughed again, but he didn't say anything. It was Liz who said, "David's dad keeps him on a tight allowance."

"Actually," David said, "he doesn't think I need a car while I'm out here, and I probably don't. I just like to have a little mobility. One of my old roommates gave the Corolla to me for two hundred bucks."

"Ooooh," Ned said. "I'm afraid you got taken on that deal."

But Ned was rather impressed that David's father didn't lavish a lot of money on the boy. He knew that he was actually a little too free with the money he gave to Liz. He had always kept a much tighter rein on his sons.

When they reached Day's Market in Heber, Ned proposed the great question of the day. As they were walking in, he said, "Here's what I'm thinking. I know the standard thing is to cook a turkey—and I'm happy to give that a shot, if that's what everyone wants. The only trouble is, they take forever to cook, and from what I hear, they're hard to get just right. Besides, I'm not much of a turkey lover. Now, on the other hand, I do admit that I am widely known throughout the western world as one of the great maestros of the barbecue grill. And I strongly believe that Thanksgiving should be designated as a health-food free zone. I could slap some steaks about two inches thick on the old grill, flip them over once, douse them in my own special Gates Sauce—which I order by the case from Kansas City—and produce a medium-rare delight. We could throw in a baked potato, easily nuked, and forget about whipping up lumpy mashed potatoes. We could even—"

"Dad . . ."

"Yes."

"David doesn't eat red meat."

"I do a little, sometimes. Just not a great big steak. But that's not a problem. We could throw on a chicken breast with the steaks and I'd be in heaven. I love barbecued stuff."

"Hey, I *rarely* eat steak," Ned said. "I was just thinking, for Thanksgiving, we could indulge a little."

"Actually, I've gotten so I don't like steak," David said, "but a chicken breast would be terrific."

Ned had enjoyed hearing about David's love of cars, combined with his father's resistance to give him one. That had all sounded good. But he wasn't going to allow anyone into his family who was finicky about eating a steak once in a while. Ned was never going to be a fanatic about that sort of thing. This was one more piece of evidence against the boy. All of Liz's brothers ate steak practically raw—and let the juices run down their chins. No way would they let someone this delicate join their table.

"Or here's another idea," David said. "Last year I did go home for Thanksgiving, and my mom cooked a turkey in one of those plastic bags they have now. I can't say I helped her all that much, but I watched her do it, and she kept saying how quick it was, and how moist the turkey came out. I'll bet we could get one of those things, and I could read the directions—and maybe call my mom—and I'd be willing to get up in the morning and start the turkey while you're out for your run. My mom also has a recipe for stuffing that's so good you say a second blessing *after* you eat, just to thank the Lord you experienced it."

*Cute. Even his jokes portray him as humble and thankful.*

Everyone had stopped in the little entry area where the shopping carts were lined up. Liz pulled a cart loose from the others, but she stopped and looked at Ned. "Dad, I think that's a better idea. I'd really miss it if we didn't have turkey for Thanksgiving—and that stuffing sounds great."

"Okay. Fine. Let's pick out a turkey. Let's get the biggest one they've got."

"Now we've hurt your feelings, haven't we?" David said.

*Oh, brother. Now Mr. Do-Right is trying to be sensitive—and in the process, making me look like a jerk in front of my daughter.*

"Hey, no. Not at all," Ned said. "That barbecue thing was a bad idea. I was just thinking like a lazy man. Let's get us a *nice* turkey and *stuff it.*"

"Daaaddd, are you sure?"

"Hey, is the Statue of Liberty a potential arsonist?"

"What?"

"Never mind. Let's get a *giant* turkey. We'll bag it, roast it, stuff it, and fall down on our knees in praise."

The three of them were still standing in place, creating a bit of an obstacle as other customers had to make their way around them. David was staring at Ned, looking confused.

"Don't worry," Liz was saying. "Dad is like this sometimes. It's called a double message. I learned about it in psychology. It's very important to ignore it, or he'll just keep it up. Call your mom so we'll know what we need for the stuffing."

"All right." David was still watching Ned, but he did reach

into his jacket pocket and pull out a tiny cell phone. He began to push buttons.

*I'm trying to remember, Ned. You've acted stupid before, but I'm not sure that you've ever reached quite this level. That was a verbal tantrum you just threw, and you know it. And all because they want a turkey and not a bunch of five-pound sirloin strips.*

*Hey, we're buying a turkey. What are you talking about?*

*I like David. The better I get to know him, the more I see in him. But you're not giving him a chance.*

*He prays* after *meals. He doesn't eat like a man. He's ashamed of himself that he likes nice cars. And he's worried that he might have hurt my feelings. I don't have to put up with stuff like that. He wants my daughter, Kate. He did everything but say so this morning.*

*I know. And it brought tears to my eyes. He really loves her.*

*Who wouldn't? That's not an accomplishment. What I want to see is a sign that the guy is normal. And so far, the only thing normal about him is his libido, which works just fine.*

*Oh, right. He held her hand.*

"Do you want to talk to Mom for a second?"

Ned was stunned. Was the kid talking to him?

But Liz was taking the phone. They had all moved inside the store but had then slipped off to the side, near the donut racks. David had been talking to his mother, expressing his joy about the warm weather. He had been listing out loud the various ingredients he would have to buy, while Liz wrote them down.

Water chestnuts. Mushrooms. Green olives. It all sounded horrifying.

Now he was letting Liz say hello, and she was calling the woman "Sister Markham," and sounding like the two knew each other very well.

"Well, I don't know," Liz said. "You mentioned that before, but I don't see how I could do that."

*What's that all about? Why have these two been talking to each other? I didn't know David existed until yesterday.*

"Well, yes, I have thought about it. And I know you're right. New England at Christmastime would be beautiful. But my brothers are all coming home. I really want to be here to see them."

Ned was suddenly in a panic. What was the woman trying to do?

"Well . . . that might be a possibility. Then I could be there for New Year's Eve. I've always wanted to be at Times Square that night. I know when you live around New York, you probably—"

Liz hesitated, and Ned's mind raced. He had to stop this.

"Oh, could we? You mean on the train? That would be so fun."

*So this is it. They're trying to kidnap my daughter on New Year's Eve. I've got to do something.*

He started forward, not quite clear what he was about to do.

And then David said, "Hey, Ned, this may be a funny way to meet my mom, but would you like to talk to her for a minute?"

Ned did it. Maybe it was an accident. Maybe he was temporarily blinded—or temporarily insane. After it happened, he couldn't remember the last seconds before the collision. All he knew was that he had crashed his cart into a tall stack of canned pumpkin pie mixes, and the structure had given way like one of those imploding buildings. It sank at first, then the top toppled, and cans rolled in all directions. The noise was terrific, the confusion frightening.

But at least Ned didn't end up saying hello to "Sister Markham."

# Chapter Four

Ned was embarrassed. He knew he had overreacted at the grocery store, knew he was overreacting in general. He really did need to calm down. So when he got home, he let David and Liz study, and he tried to do the same. He spent some time in his office staring at his scriptures, even sliding his eyes over the words, and of course, learning little, since his mind kept wandering back to everything he didn't want to think about: especially little fantasies about giving David the lovely gift of a flight home in time to have Thanksgiving with his own dear family. The boy could even take the turkey. In fact, he could stuff it—or at least take the ingredients along.

When Liz finally appeared at his office, he hoped she wouldn't say anything about the little incident with the tower of cans. But Liz never had learned to be diplomatic.

"Are you okay now, Dad?"

Ned turned in his swivel chair. "What do you mean?"

"You know. You seemed pretty upset." She sat down in Ned's leather-upholstered recliner.

"Okay. I shouldn't have chewed out that stock boy. He probably didn't make the decision to stack those cans right where someone was destined to run into them. But I'm over it now. We picked the stuff up."

"You didn't have to buy all the bent cans. The manager kept saying he didn't expect that."

Ned smiled. "But now I have a twenty-years' supply of pumpkin pie mix. If the big bomb ever drops, and we have to live on our food storage, I'm sure pumpkin pie mix will taste better than all that wheat your mother made me buy."

Liz was smiling too, but she said, "Dad, something's wrong. You're not acting like yourself. You told me you wanted to talk to me. Now might be a good time to do that."

But Ned needed two hours, not fifteen minutes, and the agreement was that they would head over to the golf course at one o'clock. So he said, "I do want to talk to you. But it wasn't anything about . . . it was just something . . . actually, let's just play golf now, and we'll talk later. Okay?"

"Okay. But Daddy, don't get too competitive. It's just for fun, and David hasn't played for a long time. Let's just go hit the ball around and enjoy ourselves."

Ned was astounded. "I don't know what you're trying to say, Liz."

She rubbed her hands along the leather of the armrests and looked off toward the bookcase, not at him. "Well, sometimes you get a little too serious about golf, don't you think?"

"I try to improve, if that's what you mean. But it's not important to me. It's just a game."

Ned was the first to admit that he had spent a lot of money over the years on the latest drivers, newly designed putters, and various devices that were supposed to "groove" a guy's swing. Kate had always teased him about that. But when he walked away from the golf course, he forgot his score—at least within a few days—and he had almost completely overcome the little swearing problem he had had at one time. Every golfer he knew uttered a four-letter word from time to time. The game was frustrating, that was all. But Ned hadn't bent a club over his knee in at least a year, and he didn't think *damn* was a swear word in the true sense anyway.

"Sometimes, you kind of change personalities when you play, Dad. Your eyes get all—"

"No, no. This is for fun today. Let's just go over and take a few last swings before winter sets in."

Half an hour later, the threesome was standing on the first tee of the Lake Course at Wasatch Mountain State Park. Ned had played the course dozens of times, and, as much as he loved it, he did harbor some rather negative feelings toward this first hole. It was a par five, but the fairway was made narrow by tall trees on the right side and a big, round willow tree on the left, and just beyond the trees was an almost right-turn dogleg. A player didn't need to blast the ball a long way, but he did have to hit the area beyond the opening in the trees so he had a good line on the second shot. With a big second shot and a good pitch, a birdie was always possible, but a mistake or two could turn the hole into a disaster.

"You go first, Brother Stevens."

Ned glanced up.

"I mean, Ned."

Ned actually didn't mind doing that. He had spent the last five minutes taking practice swings. He was ready. "Don't lash at the ball," he had been telling himself. "Just take an easy swing. Say 'Johnny' on the take-away, 'Miller' on the swing." He had attended a little workshop from Johnny Miller and had learned a trick to keep a smooth pace. He was supposed to say, "John . . . ny" as he took the club back, and "Mill . . . er" as he unleashed his swing. It was all about one-two, one-two. Nice and smooth.

Ned stepped to the tee box with the blue markers. This was the harder, longer way to play the course. He and David had already discussed that. Or actually, Ned had merely said, "I usually play the blue tees, but if you'd rather play the whites, it doesn't matter at all to me."

And David had said, "The blues are fine. I'm so rusty it probably won't matter either way."

So Ned used the ball to push his tee into the ground, and then walked back and took a look down the fairway. He tried to envision the flight of the ball. It was a trick he had learned in one of his golf books, or maybe it was from one of the golf magazines he subscribed to. He walked back to the ball, addressed it, looked down the fairway again, took a nice, smooth practice swing—John . . . ny Mill . . . er—then stepped closer. He took a long breath, regripped a couple of times, got comfortable, and then, John . . . ny, whack!

He did exactly what he had told himself not to do. He swung too hard, too quick. He had hit the ball solidly, and it took off straight, but Ned knew what was coming. The thing started to slice and then bent to the right like a boomerang. For a moment he held out some hope that he had hit the ball high and long enough to clear some big cottonwoods and end up in decent shape. But he saw it hit a tree limb and drop straight down.

"I can't believe I did that!" he shouted, mostly to himself. But he caught himself immediately and turned back to David and Liz. "I told myself to take a smooth swing, and then I jumped all over it." He reached in his pocket and pulled out another ball. "Let's just forget that one ever happened. I'll start for real this time."

"Sure. Take a Mulligan. It's the first hole," David said.

"Yeah. Go ahead, Dad."

So Ned started the routine all over. And this time he remembered the tempo. It was a nice, easy, "Johnny Miller" swing, but he might have exaggerated a little. His club struck the ground slightly behind the ball and lost a lot of its velocity. The ball flew straight but without any power. It looped down the fairway and dropped short of the dogleg. He would be stuck with taking a little lay-up shot to get around the corner or else he would have to shape the ball around the trees—slice it on purpose—and that wasn't something he could do with much consistency.

"What a rotten start," Ned said, as he looked back at David. "I haven't done that in a long time."

But Liz was quick to say, "Hey, it's just for fun today. I haven't played for months, and David hasn't either."

"That's right," David said. He was using Ned's last-year's set of clubs. The golf bag had a built-in, two-legged, stand-up device on it. David looked into the bag and thought for a moment, and then pulled out an iron.

Ned nodded. "That might be the smart thing if you haven't played for a while," he said. "A driver is hard to control when you're trying to get back into the game."

"Yeah, that's true. And actually, I'm a little worried that if I happen to connect well, I could hit the ball right on past that dogleg."

*Oh, listen to this. The big hitter. He's afraid he's going to hit it too far. Maybe this is a chance for the boy to learn a little of that humility he's so worried about.*

59

David addressed the ball and didn't bother with a practice swing. He took the club way back, almost around his head, and then let loose a huge swing. It was actually a thing of beauty, and Ned's breath caught for a moment, but he couldn't help smiling when he saw the ball hook hard to the left. David had hit it a long way, but it bent way left of the big willow tree and was gone. He would probably never find the ball.

Ned said, before David could even look back, "Go ahead, take another one. Like you said, it's the first hole."

"I'll have to take provisional, I guess. That one might be out of play."

*And then some, iron boy.*

David walked back to his bag and got another ball. Ned had set him up with a dozen new Titleists. He hated to admit it to himself, but he really hoped old David lost every one of them. It would be worth the price, just to watch.

But then Ned stopped himself. He wasn't going to take that attitude. He was going to help the young man. "David, I noticed your grip was awfully strong. I think I'd rotate that right hand back just a little."

"Yeah, I know. I saw that slice you hit, and I got thinking, I could easily do the same thing. I think I did grip the club too strong."

"Just back it off a little. You've got a nice swing."

David did just that—and it worked. He hit a beautiful shot, right down the center. It split the trees in the narrow part of the fairway and landed in a perfect spot for a second shot to the green. Ned was happy for him.

Or at least he wanted to be. He would have felt better if his own ball had been sitting in a better spot.

The agreement had been not to ride in carts, since—as Ned

always said—the point of golf was to get some exercise. But Ned's legs were still a little weary from the run that morning. He hoisted his clubs on his shoulder and walked toward the red tee markers—the women's tee box—and then he said, "Okay, Sis. Remember what I taught you. Keep your head down and just swing through the ball."

But Liz straightened up on her first try and swung right over the ball. "Strike one," she yelled, and she laughed, and then she addressed the ball again. She gave it a decent whack, but she topped the ball and it didn't go far. It got a pretty good roll and ended up about halfway to the dogleg. "Oh, man, that was terrible," she shouted to her dad. "I didn't keep my head down, did I?"

"Just remember next time."

She laughed, and they all grabbed their clubs and headed down the fairway. Liz strode out rather fast, and David walked with her. When Ned caught up to them, Liz was already getting ready for another swing. Ned set his bag down and just then heard David say, "When we tell you to keep your head down, that's a little misleading. It's not so much your head as it is the angle of your spine. As you take the club back, don't straighten up. That way the club comes through on the same plane that it's on as you take it away."

"Oh. Okay. I don't think I ever understood that."

David stepped away, and she took a practice swing. "Perfect," he said. "Just like that."

This time she caught the ball clean. It jumped off her club and almost sailed too far. "Oh, wow!" Liz shouted. "That was great. David, thank you!"

*Oh, David, thank you. Never mind who taught you the game.*

Ned grabbed his clubs and walked toward his ball. By then

he had decided he might as well take a chance. David obviously knew some basics, but he had a big, wild swing, and he probably knew nothing about shaping shots. This was a chance to show the boy a little something. Ned grabbed a 5-iron from his bag and looked over at David, who had stopped to watch. "I probably ought to pull out a short iron and lay up, but what the heck, I'm going to see if I can fade the ball around these trees. I hate to give up all chance for a par."

"Well, you're a braver man than I," David said. "I never know what's going to happen when I try something like that."

*That's right, muscle boy. You don't. But watch this.*

Ned took three practice swings, then four. He thought he had the right cut-motion to make the ball bend around the corner just enough. The only thing he had to be careful about was overdoing it and hitting a quick slice into the woods again. But it was that last thought that probably led to his mistake. He backed off just a little on what he had practiced, and when he hit the ball, he felt immediately that he had hit a perfect shot—if he had wanted to send the ball straight down the fairway. But there was very little slice in it. The ball angled past the near trees and carried across to the other side of the dogleg—and into the wrong fairway.

"Ouch," David said. "That's what I would have done."

*That's the last I want to hear from you, David.*

Ned tossed his club into his bag, and marched away. He wasn't finished yet. At least the ball was lying in a good spot. He was a long way out, but if he could get over a couple of pine trees, he had a decent line to the green. Besides, he was a killer with a 3-wood.

David walked with Liz, and Ned could see that he was talking to her again. If he wasn't careful, he was going to tell her too much and get her confused. But Liz used a fairway wood and hit the ball farther than she ever had in her life. Ned could hardly believe the shot—straight at the green with some real sting on it. She could probably get to the green with a long iron if she hit the ball that well again.

Then David walked back to his ball and got out a wood. He stood at the ball, seeming a little too relaxed. He gazed toward the green for a moment, then took a nice, slow backswing. His swing was all flow, but powerful, and the sound of the club against the ball was like a rifle shot. Ned was up the fairway a little, on the left, and when the ball passed by, he heard the sound of sucking wind—the sound he had heard once when he had seen Tiger Woods play, live. The ball stayed in the air for minutes, not seconds, it seemed. It floated on and on, rising much longer than seemed possible. It was a gigantic shot, but toward the end, it drifted a little to the right, took a bad kick, and dribbled into the sand trap on the right side of the green.

"Holy cow!" Liz was yelling. "That was a *missile*. That thing went *forever!*"

*Okay, okay. He smashed it. And he hit it fairly straight. Like he'll do that twice in one day.*

"But it ended up in the sand," Ned heard David say. "I'm not very good with a sand wedge."

Ned wasn't going to listen to the guy talk anymore. He was just going to play his game. He got out a 3-wood and hit the ball as hard as he could. He caught it clean, feeling that wonderful twang when the sweet spot of a metal wood connects with a golf ball. It flew over the pine trees, hung in the air, then settled onto the fairway—the correct one this time—about sixty yards short of David's missile shot. Or maybe seventy. Eighty, at most.

But it was okay. Ned had just made a great shot, and both Liz and David were yelling to him that he had hit a bomb of his own. Now, he just had to hit a good pitch to the green. If he could hit the ball close to the hole, he would still have a shot at beating David.

*I'm going to do it. I'm going to show that boy. These kids can hit the ball hard, and when they happen to keep it in the fairway, they look good, but when it comes to the short game, they have no touch at all.*

Ned waited for Liz, who hit another nice shot, a long iron blast that rolled to the edge of the green. She could putt from there. Ned didn't think she had ever played this hole so well. All his work with her was finally paying off.

He stopped at his ball, got out a pitching wedge, and then he talked to himself. He envisioned what he wanted to do. He had plenty of green to work with. It was just a matter of lifting a soft shot to the green and letting the ball roll back to the hole. There was a natural left-break to the green that wasn't that obvious if a guy hadn't played the hole many times.

He addressed the ball, felt the tension, and stepped away. *Settle down. Nice and easy.* He stepped back up, swung a couple of times, and then did almost exactly what he wanted to do. The ball looped to the green, landing a little short of where he had pictured it, but it rolled well and drifted to the left, as he knew it would. It was a good shot, but it had come up a little short—a good twelve feet from the hole. Still, with a good putt, Ned could make par, and David was in the sand. If he got out all right, he could probably two-putt and match Ned, but considering how things had started, Ned could live with that.

"Great shot!" David was shouting.

*You got that right. The ol' guy still has some game in him.*

Liz was lining up her putt, and Ned wanted to tell her about the break in the green, but David was there ahead of him. "Did you see what your dad's ball did? It broke to the left quite a bit—at least a foot. So picture the arc your ball will have to make and pick a spot on the green, in that arc. Then just roll the ball across that spot."

Liz was listening carefully, nodding, taking all of this very seriously. Ned had never seen her look so intense.

*He's going to ruin the game for her. She's always just had fun at it.*

But she stroked the ball nicely. It rolled toward the hole, drifted left, and slipped on by, just to the right. But she had left herself only about a foot and a half, coming back. She ran to the ball, knocked it in the hole, and then jumped straight in the air. "That was a *six,* David! Even after that bad drive. I could have had a par if I'd started out better."

David seemed to forget all about his next shot. He hustled toward Liz as she ran to him. They slapped hands, up high, and then she threw her arms around him. "I'm *good!* I can't believe how good I am."

*Okay. Okay. Now step back and let go of the guy.*

"Honey, that was a great putt," Ned said.

But Liz didn't seem to hear, or if she did, she didn't say so. She was still making a big deal out of the tips David was giving her. Ned thought about that first year in Provo, when Ned hadn't known anyone, and his sons were all gone from home. That was when Ned had taught Liz to play golf, and she had probably played with him more than she really wanted to. One day up at the Hobble Creek course, she had missed the green on a par three, but had hit a little chip shot that had rolled into the hole. It was her first birdie—maybe her only birdie—and that day she had run to Ned and thrown her arms around him. He couldn't have been more happy if he had knocked in an eagle putt of his own.

David finally remembered that the game was still going on, and he walked to the sand trap. Ned looked back to see if any golfers were behind them, getting tired of all this carrying on over a bogey, but there were very few people on the course today and no one behind them.

Ned could see that David was going to have trouble. His ball was in close to the lip of the sand trap, and he had very little green to work with, the flag being so close. It was a tough shot.

But David didn't take a lot of time. He swung through the ball and lifted it very high. There was a spray of sand, and for a moment, the ball seemed to be arching too long, but it dropped, almost hit the pin, then trickled barely past it. It stopped about six inches from the hole.

*How did he do that?*

"David! What a shot!" Liz shouted. "I thought you weren't good at sand shots."

*Yeah. Exactly.*

But David was blushing. Literally, blushing. "I'm not, usually. I really lucked out. Sometimes, when you don't expect much, you relax and take the right kind of stroke."

*Yeah, yeah, yeah.*

The only thing Ned knew was that David had a birdie, and he had beaten Ned on the first hole. Still, Ned knew this green, and he rolled a perfect putt. It broke about six inches and dropped into the heart of the hole.

"Wow! What a beautiful putt," David was saying. "You've got a great stroke."

"Well, at least I saved my par," Ned said. "I expected a lot worse after I duffed my drive."

"Dad, what are you talking about? You were great. I've seen you mess up this hole lots of times."

*Thanks, Liz.*

"Well, anyway, a birdie, a par, and a bogey," Ned said. "That's not bad on this hole." He picked up his clubs and started toward the second tee.

"Actually, Ned, I had a par, the same as you," David said.

Ned stopped and turned around. "What are you talking about?"

"I took that provisional shot, but I don't take Mulligans."

*What? You set me up! You told me to take a Mulligan.* "Oh. Well, if you're not taking one, I won't either."

"No, no. It's fine. Go ahead, if that's what you and your friends normally do. It's actually kind of selfish, the reason I don't do it. I don't want to do anything that inflates my handicap. I'd rather have a pure number."

"Why do you worry about a handicap?"

"Well . . . I don't that much anymore. But I used to play in tournaments once in a while, and I just got in the habit of always keeping a strict count. I feel a little better about it that way."

*So what am I? A cheater?*

"I'll put a five down for you and a six for me," Ned said.

"No, Daddy," Liz told him. "Just count your strokes the way you always do."

"I only take one Mulligan a round. That's what most people do. It's not like I'm taking 'do-overs' every hole."

"Yeah," David said. "That is what most people do. In fact,

for today, since we're just out here for fun, go ahead and put me down for a four. What the heck?"

"I'll tell you what," Ned said. "I'll put you down for nothing at all. We can each keep our own score—in our heads. We're just having fun. It's not like we're competing with each other."

"Come on, Dad. Don't get mad."

"Mad? What are you talking about?"

"I don't know. You just sounded sort of . . . never mind."

Ned walked on to the second tee and, in the gentlest of voices, said, "Go ahead, David. You take the honors. You go first."

David nodded, walked to the tee box and placed his ball, and looked down the fairway. "This is a dogleg to the left, isn't it?" he asked.

"Yeah," Liz said. "See, there's the green down there."

The hole was similar to the first one, with an opposite dogleg, but there was an opening, so the green was visible from the tee box, and it was a shorter hole, a par four. David looked the situation over and seemed to consider for a time. Then he asked, "Do you think it's possible to cut this corner and go straight at the green?"

*Are you kidding?*

"Not really, David," Ned said. "That's a long shot."

"Well, we're just having fun. I think I'll pull out my driver and see what I can do with it."

*Good. This is where a boy makes a mistake and loses to a man. There's no way you can hit the ball that far.*

And then he did.

He set up on an angle, aiming toward the green, and launched a shot that was long and high. The ball was a spot in the sky that seemed to hang there forever. When it dropped, it settled right in front of the green. Ned was a little afraid he might start to cry, just watching such beauty. And Liz sounded absolutely reverent when she said, "I can't believe it. David, you are *so* good."

"I'm just loose because it's not a tournament or anything. When I played for BYU, I wouldn't have even tried something like that."

*You played for BYU?*

Ned was numb. He hardly thought about his shot, but he hit the ball pretty well—for an old man. He picked up his bag, and then tried to sound casual when he said, "I didn't realize you played college golf. I don't think you mentioned that."

"Well, it was a long time ago," David said. "Before my mission. At first I decided not to play college sports, and I didn't have a scholarship or anything, but I missed competing at *something*. So I walked on that year, and I made the team."

"But you must have played a lot before that."

"Not really. I played some junior golf, and our coach always said I had a good, natural swing, but I was so busy in other sports, I didn't give much time to it. I was lucky to make the team at BYU, with no scholarship, but once I did, I improved a lot. I was actually getting so I was playing fairly well before my mission. But when I got back I just figured I needed to put all my time into school, so I didn't go back to the team, and I don't play much now. I thought I was going to make a fool of myself today, playing with someone as good as you are."

*I don't hate you. Hate is wrong. But if I ever do decide to hate anyone, I'm going to keep you in mind for the job.*

They stopped at the women's tee box, and Liz got out her driver, but before she turned toward the ball, she said, "I'll tell you what's funny, Dad. David says he had to worry about school, and that's why he couldn't play golf, but he's never had a grade lower than an A. Never, ever."

*What a surprise.*

"Hey, that's not true," David said. "I don't know who told you that, but it's not true."

"Your mom told me. And she wouldn't lie."

"Well, she's wrong." David had kept his bag on his shoulder, but he set it down now. He was smiling a little, even though he was clearly trying not to.

"When didn't you get an A?"

"It doesn't matter. What my mom said isn't true. I ought to know."

"So what was your bad grade?"

"I got a B one time."

"In what?"

The smile was getting bigger. "It doesn't matter."

*Let's just play golf. Okay?*

"It never happened," Liz challenged.

"Yes, it did."

"What class? If you can't tell me, it didn't happen."

"Wood shop."

Liz cracked up. "Wood shop? When?"

But now David couldn't help grinning with those lovely white teeth and that cute, red-faced blush of his. "Junior high."

"That doesn't count."

"You said I'd never had anything but A's, and I told you it's not true. I did get a B."

Liz spun toward her dad. "He may have gotten a B in shop, but you know what he did? He built a playhouse for his sisters out in his backyard, and he even wired it so they had lights out there. It was really fancy, with an upstairs and downstairs, a bunk bed, and the whole thing. His sisters worship him. They're always telling me about things he's done for them."

Ned couldn't resist asking, "So when did you meet his sisters, Liz?"

"One of them goes to the Y. And his parents come out here a lot. They brought his younger sister out last time, and we all had dinner together. Everyone embarrassed David almost to death, telling all the great things he's done. I didn't know about any of that stuff before then. David never tells me what he's done. I didn't know until just now that he played golf for BYU."

"You better go ahead and take your swing, Liz."

She glanced back toward the first fairway. "It's okay. There's no one behind us."

"I know, but—"

"What's so amazing is how many *kinds* of things he can do. I mean, it's one thing to be a brain, but he can *fix* anything. Everyone in his family tells stories about how he can take things apart, figure them out, and make them work. I mean, me, I can't do anything like that. I'm like you, Dad. When something stops working, the only thing I know how to do is check the plug."

David rolled his eyes as though he were put out by all the praise. He was still blushing. "Just hit the ball, Liz," he said. "You don't know about all the things I took apart and couldn't put back together."

"Ooooh," Liz said. "Another dark secret, like your B in wood shop."

"No. Like my secret life as a serial killer. That's the part of my life I usually don't mention."

Actually, Ned was interested in hearing more about that.

71

# Chapter Five

All in all, the round of golf ended better than it had begun. Ned actually played well—better than he had for a long time. He realized early that he couldn't beat David, so he didn't try. That seemed to help him play relaxed, and he hit the ball well. Besides, David managed to get himself into more than a little trouble. He was hitting the ball long, but he wasn't all that consistent. He was like Tiger Woods at saving himself, with big hits from the rough, but his score—although no one kept track officially—wasn't all that much better than Ned's. One really great moment—for Ned—happened when David overestimated the distance he could hit an 8-iron, and hit the ball into a pond on a par three. By the time he was finished, he had taken a double bogey on the hole while Ned was making a nice two-putt par. A guy had to feel good about that. Ned would have been even happier if David had lost his temper and maybe let a bad word slip, but that never happened. In fact, in a voice over-flowing with sincerity, he told Ned, "That was a beautiful putt. You really know these greens, don't you?"

Of course, Ned knew what David was implying: The kid fig-ured, since Ned played this course all the time, his "local knowl-edge" gave him an advantage. What a boob! Why couldn't he act like a man and just admit that Ned was a wizard with a put-ter in his hands?

After the game, the three drove back to the house. David and Liz headed off in separate directions to study, and Ned, after a shower, sat in the great room and read the newspaper. It was a good strategic location where he could spot either party, if any sort of tryst was attempted. That didn't happen, but about the time Ned started to think about cooking something for dinner—or talking Liz into doing it—the two showed up, almost at the same time, both cleaned up and looking sparkly. "Dad," Liz announced, "David and I have to run down to Provo. We're invited to a wedding reception."

"Oh, really? You didn't mention that."

"Didn't I? I'm sorry. It's for one of David's really good friends. We feel like we have to go."

Liz was the worst liar Ned had ever known. When she was a little girl, she would get halfway through a lie, suddenly break down and sob, and admit to everything. Ned half expected her to do that now. She was standing in front of him, but she was looking over his head, speaking stiffly. And the dead giveaway was David. He had turned away and was looking off across the room, his face as pink as a baby's bottom.

Ned started to panic. What were they going to do? He took a long look at David, waited until the boy finally looked at him, and then asked, as "knowingly" as he could, "So who is this friend who's getting married?"

"Oh, it's Jeff . . . uh . . . Johnson."

"Jeffa Johnson?"

"No. Just Jeff. Jeff Johnson." By now he was shading toward hot pink.

"Where's the reception being held?"

But it was Liz who answered. "It's at a reception center."

"Could you be a little more specific than that?"

"Excuse me?"

"I'd just like to know where you're going. You know, in case of an emergency." Ned felt a little heat in his own face. But he enjoyed watching them squirm.

"I'm not sure, Dad. It's close to campus. It's on the invitation."

"What invitation?"

"It's in David's car."

There was a long pause, and Ned almost asked her to go get it, but suddenly Liz remembered. "Oh, yeah. It's called 'The Old Chapel.' It's an old Mormon church. Jeff is marrying a girl named Allison Wheatley."

Ned didn't know whether he was bothered more by her awkward lying or by this sudden burst of confidence. Either way, he still didn't believe her story. But they were edging toward the stairway now, and Ned decided not to push things any further. The fact was, if they wanted to sneak off and be alone, and leave him home by himself all evening, who was he to stop them? He was alone most of the time anyway, and they were probably together every night—being "friends." Never mind that Liz had promised to spend the holiday at home. Never mind that Ned hadn't eaten. Never mind that some things really hurt.

He did ask, "Aren't you going to eat?"

"Sure. We'll get a sandwich or something," Liz said. She glanced at David. "Or a salad." Then she asked Ned, "Can you manage for yourself?"

"I always do. Don't worry about me."

"Dad, I'm sorry. We won't be late. And David and I will cook the whole dinner tomorrow. It's going to be a nice day."

She took another step toward the stairs, and then she turned back. "And Dad, we'll have that talk. The holiday is really just beginning."

Ned stood and looked carefully at Liz, telling her with his eyes to pay attention. Then he said, "Liz, be careful. Be very, very careful."

"Oh, we will," David said. "My old car won't go fast enough to put us in any danger."

*Thanks, David. That makes me feel so much better. It's when the car stops that I get worried.*

But they left. They had lied, and now they were gone. Ned felt sick.

*So what do you think of him now, oh trusting one? And don't try to tell me they're not up to something.*

*They probably just want a little time alone, since you chaperoned them the whole time last night.*

*I think you're exactly right about that. But you tell me, what do they want to do together?*

*Have some time for each other. Go out on a date. Maybe kiss a little. What do you think two kids in love are going to do?*

*Okay. Now you've admitted it. They're not just friends, are they?*

*No. Anyone can see that. They're nuts about each other. And he probably started kissing her weeks ago.*

*Yes. Just the way we did. You were the make-out king, as I recall. What was it your friends called you? Mr. Moves?*

*Oh, come on. Don't make things up. We were serious by the time I kissed you.*

*On the second date?*

*Things went fast. Two weeks later, I asked you to marry me.*

*Then don't be surprised if Liz has a ring for Christmas. What?*

*You heard me. David is going to be your son-in-law. And you're going to have beautiful, smart grandkids who are going to play better golf than you do.*

*That's unkind, Kate. Really unkind. I never thought you'd treat me that way—especially now, when I'm passing through such a dark time.*

*Just a minute. I'll get someone to play some sad music for you. Would you like cellos and French horns? There's something so plaintive about a French horn.*

Ned decided not to talk to her. She was getting cruel now. But she couldn't be dismissed quite that easily.

*I don't see how you could ask for a better son-in-law, or for better genes to mix with your own. He's going to upgrade the quality of your progeny.*

*Not if I can stop it, he's not. Liz may be impressed with all that slickness, but sooner or later she's going to see through him.*

*First of all, she's almost as old as I was when we got married, and—*

*She's flighty, Kate. She doesn't know what she wants out of life. In another few years, when she's got her feet under her, then she should start thinking about marriage.*

*It's not going to happen that way, Ned. She'll be married by August, if not by June.*

*Kate, as I recall, it's against the rules for you to haunt me all the time.*

*Cute, Ned. Really cute. And that's fine. I'll go now, but this is my warning—and I'd advise you not to forget it. It's stupid to try to talk Liz out of loving David. If he's "too good to be true," as you keep claiming, she'll find out. But if you try to convince her of that, she'll only like him more. That's how things have always worked and always will.*

*Oh, really? I've heard that some children listen to their parents. But then, I have some old-fashioned notions about things.*

*Ned, I'm serious. We've taught her well. If he's not all he seems to be, she'll know.*

*He's taught her to lie, Kate. They wanted out of here, and they didn't have the courage to say why.*

*Trust them, Ned. If they weren't telling the truth, they had a good reason. I feel sure of it.*

*Maybe you better check with some of your superiors about that. Last I heard, sin was sin. I sure hope you got sent to a place where that's true.*

*Watch it, bub. I know where I can get thunderbolts tossed your way.*

Just then Ned heard a terrific rumble, and for a moment he thought it *was* thunder. He was relieved when he realized it was just a truck going by. But once the noise subsided, he was left feeling very much alone. He put his paper down and walked out to the deck. He watched the edge of the woods for a time, but no deer were around tonight. The valley seemed gloomy, with the sun mostly gone and the mountains so gray. He wasn't sure what to do with himself. He had planned to eat with the kids, or even drive them over to Park City for another dinner out. He couldn't bear the thought of watching television, and though he normally would have done some reading on a night like this, he didn't feel like doing that.

He couldn't seem to get past the thought that Liz wanted to be with David tonight—and not at home. He tried to tell himself that he was worried about what they might be doing, but that fear didn't hold up very well. He knew Liz too well for that, he thought, and ol' David—in spite of what Ned had been telling Kate—just didn't seem very dangerous. Liz apparently liked to be with David. By now David was probably entertaining her with a fascinating discussion about humility and how he had acquired it. What fun!

But even sarcasm didn't help. The fact was, Liz had chosen David tonight, not her dad. She was gradually but deliberately giving her life away, turning it over to a boy who thought that he was well on his way to heaven. Ned had always known that she would get married, but why couldn't she bring home some "regular guy"—someone who knew how to enjoy a good steak, who didn't know which end of a golf club to pick up, who didn't realize yet that he needed to exercise, who didn't know for sure what he wanted to do with his life and appreciated a little advice? A man could put his arm around a boy like that and maybe guide him a little, bring him into the family and help him become, in time, worthy of the honor. But how could a man warm up to Zeus, for crying out loud?

Maybe Kate was right. Maybe Liz was hooked on David and was going to marry him no matter what anyone said. And just maybe Ned needed to back off and try to like the boy. But the very thought of doing that ticked him off. He suddenly felt angry about the hand that life had dealt him. He needed to let off some steam, so he got in his car and drove to Heber, walked into Wendy's, and ordered the bacon cheeseburger combo—

with two patties of ground-up red meat—then had the whole thing Biggie-Sized. He got the big Sprite, with sugar, and enough fries to fill up every artery with sludge. And he wasn't finished yet. He drove straight from Wendy's to Granny's and ordered one of their giant milkshakes—chocolate with Oreo cookies mixed in. He came close to ordering a Coke besides, but he was still sloshing from all that Sprite.

Then he took the long way home, out Highway 40 to River Road. There was always a better chance of seeing deer along that road, but there were none tonight. By the time he got home, the milkshake, on top of all that other food, was starting to make him sick, and he was no longer angry, just depressed. He dumped most of the milkshake down the kitchen sink and decided he might as well use the evening to prepare for his Sunday School class.

He actually got wrapped up in some background material he had downloaded from GospeLink, and the time passed quickly, but eventually he started to wonder how long this wedding reception could last—or more accurately, how long the kids thought they could pull off their little ruse. If they had any shame at all, they couldn't stay out very late.

But not so. It was after ten o'clock before they finally came wandering in, and by then Ned was ready to blow their cover and just challenge them straight out. But they had gotten their story together this time. They had seen a lot of good friends, and then someone had asked them to join them for ice cream. (Apparently, David wasn't quite the health nut he claimed to be, if you bought this story.) What worried Ned the most was that Liz told the story much more smoothly this time—except that she still couldn't make eye contact. The girl was getting better at duping her father, and that was scary.

Ned gave Liz a cold stare, but he didn't challenge her story, and then the kids went downstairs to watch another movie. Ned didn't even bother to join them.

*Let them snuggle, if that's what they want to do. Let them kiss each other, right in my own basement.*

He just hoped that when this fling with danger was over, Liz would come to her senses.

Ned watched the end of the news in his bedroom, and then went to bed. A cold front was supposed to be moving in, and all this Indian summer weather was about to end. Ned decided he'd better run the canyon one last time in the morning before the first snow came. He just hoped *marathon boy* wouldn't get up at three—or whatever time it had been that morning—so he could prance all the way to the top.

But Ned had eaten a little too late and had certainly eaten too much. He didn't really settle down until past midnight, and at six in the morning he was sound asleep. It was around six-thirty when he heard a noise in the house. His first thought was that it was the middle of the night and David and Liz were still up. But he was hearing little clanks coming from the kitchen. Were the two having a late-night snack?

Ned pulled himself out of bed and walked to his bedroom door. He stared toward the big, open kitchen area, but he saw only David, by himself. He was standing next to the sink, looking down at the island countertop, and he seemed intent on some sort of project that involved cutting with a large knife. "What time is it?" Ned mumbled.

David looked up. "Oh, I'm sorry. I was trying to be quiet so I wouldn't wake you."

"What are you doing?"

"I thought I better get started on our dinner. That bag

speeds up the cooking time on the turkey a whole lot, but this stuffing is kind of complicated, and I've never tried to cook so many things all at the same time—you know, potatoes and yams and corn and all the rest. There's also a salad to make, and I don't really know how to make gravy. I got thinking about it when I woke up this morning, and I decided I wouldn't have time to run the canyon. Is that what you're going to do?"

Ned felt as though a sumo wrestler had been sleeping on top of him all night. His stomach still hurt and his head was all full of fuzziness. "Yeah. Maybe." He thought about it for a moment. "Maybe not." And then he added, "You don't have to cook the whole meal."

"I know. I just wanted to try. It sounded kind of fun. And then, I know that you and Liz are trying to find some time to have a chat. I thought, if I cooked, you two could get away for a while—maybe go for a walk. I feel like I'm intruding on your time together, and I'm really sorry about that."

"David, it's your vacation too. You can relax a little."

"I feel like that's all I've done. I didn't study nearly as long as I needed to yesterday."

Ned walked to the kitchen. He knew he looked like the victim of a motorcycle/eighteen-wheeler collision in his old pajamas, and with his hair probably sticking straight up, but he needed to ask this boy a question. If he had been fully awake, he probably wouldn't have done it, but with his brain still filled with fuzz, he just blurted it out. "David, do you feel like you have to be perfect or something? Don't you ever act like a normal human being?"

When Ned got his eyes in focus, he realized that David was staring at him, looking crushed. The boy was wearing an old flannel shirt and some jeans, and he still had a little "bed head" of his own. But he looked as though Ned had caught him stealing the silverware. It took him at least ten seconds to get a word out, and with each second Ned felt more ashamed for what he had asked. But he let the question stand.

"Brother Stevens, I'm human. I'm way too human."

"I'm just saying that you don't have to reach perfection *today*. Go ahead and give yourself a couple hundred years. If you get there too soon, what are you going to do with the rest of eternity?"

"I know what you're talking about. I know the impression I give. But I have more problems than most people. I'm greedy. I'm self-centered. And I have this huge ego. I spend my whole life competing, and I don't think that's what Christ expects of us. That's what I was trying to talk about yesterday. The reason I worry so much about humility is that I don't have any."

Now Ned was the one staring, not able to come up with anything.

"That 8-iron I tried to hit across the pond yesterday—that was a good example. I always think I can—"

"That's your idea of a fault? That you underclubbed a golf shot?"

"No. Not exactly. But it's symbolic of the kind of person I am."

"Give me something real. Tell me one struggle you're having. Tell me something you can't do better than all the rest of us."

"I'm forgetful, Brother Stevens. I—"

"I told you not to call me that."

"See. I forgot."

"Oh, come on. I forgot Kate's name one time when I was

introducing her. And we'd been married fifteen years. That's not a fault. That's a glitch."

"Okay. But I *am* self-centered, and I am prideful. So I concentrate on my weaknesses, and I work on them. For some reason, that really seems to bother people. You're not alone, Brother Stevens. Lots of people don't like me."

Ned couldn't do this anymore. He felt as though he were shooting a bazooka at Bambi. The boy was about to cry. "Look, never mind," Ned said. "I'm cranky in the mornings."

"It's okay. I really think we can be friends once we get to know each other better. And Brother . . . Ned . . . I love your daughter. I—"

"Stop right there. I don't want to hear it. My daughter is still a kid. Don't even think of thinking what you're thinking. I'm going to take a shower, wake up a little, and then I'm pulling Liz out of bed. I do need to talk to her."

Ned was as good as his word—except that he took his time. He knew if he got Liz up too early she was worse than he was about crankiness. He needed to have this talk, but he needed to calm down and do it right. So he took a long shower, shaved and dressed, and was getting ready to wait for a time when he heard the downstairs shower running. She was up early for the second morning in a row, and that was deeply disturbing.

*Just when you think you know someone, she starts changing all the rules on you.*

He gave her time to get ready, but he slipped down to the family room so he could catch her before she got upstairs where she could fall under David's influence. She came walking out in a worn-out chambray shirt and sweat pants. No makeup. Her hair still wet. "Daddy? What are you doing down here?"

"Waiting for you. We need to talk."

"Okay. David suggested that you and I could take some time together this morning. Just let me run upstairs and make sure he's found everything. I can hear him up there working like a demon."

*Like an angel, actually.*

"He's doing fine. He and I already had a little chat. Why don't we just get in the car and take a drive?"

"Okay." But she was hesitating. She felt her hair.

"Go dry it, if you need to."

"No. That's okay. Let's just go. I can tell something's wrong."

So they walked out to the garage, and Ned hit the button that opened the garage door. Then they piled into the Land Rover, and Ned backed out. As soon as he shifted gears and started forward, however, he said, "I just got in a bit of an argument with David."

"Argument?"

"Well . . . he didn't argue. I did. He told me he loved you, and before he could say the rest, I told him to stop. Now you tell me, Liz, how serious is this thing getting?" Ned turned down Cari Lane, heading for River Road. He didn't know where he was going, but he figured they might be gone quite a while.

"I really like him, Dad. You can tell that, I'm sure."

"That doesn't answer my question."

"First, tell me why you're mad. I don't understand what's going on."

"I'm mad because Chef Boyardee, up there in our kitchen, wants to marry you, and you're not old enough to get married. And while I'm at it, let me also mention that you told me you were bringing a *friend* home. How can you be so . . . interested

. . . in a guy when you've never even mentioned his name to me before?"

"Actually, there *is* a reason for that. First, I've dated him for a couple of months now, but I only realized how much I . . . cared about him . . . these last two weeks or so. And second, I was afraid if I told you how much I liked him, you'd get upset." She waited until he glanced over at her. "I don't know where I got that idea."

Ned heard the edge in Liz's voice and realized he'd better be careful. If this turned into a fight, he was going to lose.

"So what are you thinking, that you want to marry him?"

Liz didn't answer. She had crossed her arms and was staring straight ahead. Ned had decided that he would drive to Kamas and maybe loop around by Park City, if the conversation seemed to be lasting that long. He finally had to turn and look at Liz before she said, "I'm not quite sure yet, Dad. But I'm pretty sure that I do want to marry him."

"And when were you going to tell me?"

"I brought him up here this weekend so you could get to know him without my saying much about him. I wanted you to tell me what you thought about him."

"Okay, I will. I don't like him. Does that make any difference?"

"How can you not like him, Dad? He's so—"

"Perfect?"

"No, he's not perfect. But he's wonderful, and he's good."

"Yes, I think he mentioned that. But he tells me that he still has a big ego. By next week or so he'll get that conquered, and then he'll be perfect."

"What did you say to him?"

"I told him you're too young to get married. And you are."

Liz fiddled with the heater for a moment and turned on the fan, but the air that began to blow wasn't warm yet. She was still clasping her arms around her middle, but now she was looking out the side window. He knew she was mad, but he hoped he could at least get her to see that she ought to wait for a while, maybe let David get in a year or two of med school while she grew up some more. That was reasonable—and besides, by then, she'd be sick to death of the guy. Ned had no doubt about that.

When Liz finally spoke, she used a measured, careful tone. "I've always said I wanted to wait until I'm at least twenty-five to get married. I wanted to get out of college and then do a few things—maybe go to grad school."

"You better add a few years. You won't finish your under-graduate work until you're twenty-five."

Liz ignored him. "I wanted to have some years of fun before I settled down. But when you meet the right guy, I don't think it makes sense to pass up the chance. A lot of girls would like to get their hands on David."

"Maybe he wouldn't mind getting *his* hands on a whole lot of *them.*"

"Oh, Dad, you don't know David if you say that. I thought he was never going to kiss me. I finally had to stop at my doorstep and force the issue. He still thinks we ought to kiss only once each time we go out."

Ned was happy to hear that—for a moment—but then the other truth was obvious. "Okay," Ned said, "that's part of what I'm talking about. This guy is not normal. When something looks too good to be true, it probably is."

"That's exactly what I thought. That's what I didn't like about him at first. When school started this fall, he was in my ward, and I thought he was so good-looking. But he seemed a little too slick, if you know what I mean."

"I do know what you mean."

"And in my Sunday School class, he kept saying these amazingly idealistic things. I just thought he was way too sweet."

"Sometimes first impressions are right."

"Come on, Dad. Trust me a little. I'm not stupid. After we went out for a while, I kept finding out, he's just a very good person."

"You forgot to mention angelic, flawless, impeccable, and irreproachable."

Liz took her time, and when she spoke, she was clearly trying to control her irritation. "He's a good person, Dad. And you know what? Believe it or not, I've come to believe that isn't such a terrible trait. I'm not sure a bunch of weaknesses would improve him all that much." She bent around and made Ned look at her, and then she smiled at him.

But Ned refused. "Hey, if he's for real, that's great. I'm all for righteousness. It's self-righteousness I can't stand." Ned had stopped at the light, at Highway 40. When it changed, he drove on across and onto the Kamas road.

"I agree. After my first date, I told my roommate the same thing. I said, 'This guy is bucking to make GA by the time he's thirty.' But I gradually changed my mind. Every time we went out I liked him better."

"I don't question that the guy knows how to sell himself. That's what he's all about."

"Dad, stop it!"

Ned looked over. Liz was pointing a finger at him.

"That's not fair. You have no right to judge him without knowing him better."

"I also have no obligation to buy into him until I know a lot more. He's cute as can be, but he's—"

"He's not just good-looking. He's smart. He's motivated. He's going to have a great future. But he's a million other things. I keep discovering more and more that I like about him."

"Right. He can fix your toaster."

"Yes, he can. And that's nice. But he's a genius with computers, and I had no idea about that until last week. Then it was his roommate who told me. And you ought to see the way he treats his family—especially his little sisters."

"I'm sure his dog loves him too."

"Okay, Dad. Good point. I really wish he had a criminal record—just a couple of felonies to show he's human. His big fault is, he's trying as hard as he knows how to be a really good person, and he's trying not to be too proud of himself when he's got more talents than anyone I've ever met. A girl has got to be leery about stuff like that."

Ned suddenly braked and pulled off the road. Then he made a U-turn and headed back toward home, going much too fast. "There's no point in talking to you right now, Liz. You've let this guy snow you. But I'm going to find out more about him. Just don't make any commitments yet. I'm going to do some research."

"Dad, what are you talking about?"

"When a guy presents himself to the world as nature's most perfect product, then he can't be too surprised if the FDA steps in and does a little checking. I'm going to ask a few questions in the right places, and if he's as faultless as he thinks he is, fine. But if he's not, I want you to know it before you take one more step down the slippery slope you're standing on."

"I thought your problem with him was that he didn't have any faults. When you dig some up, won't that mean you'll like him better?"

"You're not funny."

Ned was back to Highway 40, but he hit a green light this time and hurried on through. He knew he was going way too fast, but he didn't want to talk anymore. Liz was finding ways to make him—her own father—sound as if all his impulses were wrong. Ned didn't want to talk again until he could put his evidence on the table.

"Dad, what's wrong? I thought you were doing better, but honestly, I think you're going off the deep end. I feel like you're clinging to me. You wouldn't like *any* guy I brought home, no matter who he was."

"That's not true at all. I didn't make up my mind about David until I met him. It took at least five seconds before I didn't like him, and it took a couple of hours before I knew for sure that I would never let him slither his way into my family."

Ned knew he had gone over the line with that one. But Liz didn't explode. She stared ahead, silent, for at least five minutes. Ned thought of apologizing the whole time, but he couldn't bring himself to do it.

"Dad," Liz finally said, "we haven't talked yet. You told me there were things on your mind that you needed to discuss with me. What is it you've been thinking about?"

"It isn't important—not compared to this."

"I love you, Dad."

Ned didn't want that. He preferred his anger for the moment.

"I won't agree to marry David until I'm really, really sure. But I do have to make up my own mind."

89

"I'm not so sure that's true. You're a little girl in a lot of ways. You've never been able to make up your mind about much of anything. And now you're letting him decide for you. All I'm asking is that I get some input. At the very least, you ought to take my instincts into account. I'm feeling very bad vibes about David, and you ought to be willing to grant the possibility that I'm getting some inspiration for our family."

"Okay. I do grant that. But be nice to him. Don't make this a bad day—and a bad weekend. Do what I did. Get to know him better, and give him a chance."

*I'll give him a chance, all right. I'll get the goods on him and then see what he has to say for himself.*

*Ned! You're losing it. Do you know that? You're seriously losing it.*

*Leave me alone.*

Ned drove home and parked in the garage. He yanked the car door handle and was about to bail out when Liz grabbed his arm. He looked back at her and saw that she was crying. "Dad, I love you. I'm sorry I brought David home without giving you more of a warning what was happening between us. And I will take your advice seriously."

Ned nodded. This sounded better. "Liz, do you remember that boy who kept hanging around our house in California—the one who rode the motorcycle?"

"Jason Alford?"

"I don't know his name. The one who always ate all our Oreos."

"Yeah. Jason Alford. What about him?"

"I told you to stay away from him, and it turned out, I was right. He ended up getting into a lot of trouble."

"Dad, he got picked up for toilet papering somebody's house."

"That's what he said. But he was caught climbing over a fence and—"

"Dad, I was sixteen. I didn't care anything about him."

"I'm just saying, I've always tried to watch out for you—and you've always paid attention. Until now."

Liz reached for him, touched the back of his neck. "Daddy, I know you're going through a terrible time. I'm sorry."

Ned wanted to tell her that that was not the point, that he was fine. But he couldn't get the words out.

"You need someone, Dad. All this time you spend alone just isn't healthy for you. I wish you would—"

"Liz, I don't want to have that conversation again. I'm fine."

He glanced her way, and he could see in her eyes that she didn't believe him. No one did. He took a deep breath and said, "Honey, I'm sorry. I'm just trying to protect you."

"I know."

He patted her still-wet hair, and then she leaned over and kissed him on the cheek. That made him feel better. If only he didn't have to walk upstairs now and face *stuffing boy*.

# Chapter Six

Ned walked upstairs, but he avoided David and went straight to his bedroom. Then he spent some time talking to himself. Kate was pressing him with her opinions, but he told her he needed to think things out alone. He took a while to get his head on straight, but he came to the conclusion that he had been going about everything in the wrong way. David probably wasn't such a terrible guy. He was annoying, wouldn't fit into Ned's family at all—and was *not* right for Liz—but he was probably entirely adequate for some other man's daughter. Ned knew he had to be fair about that. It was only natural that a young girl could be blinded, momentarily, since David was, after all, good-looking, rich, athletic, talented, and on his way to med school. True, Ned wanted to do some research to get beyond these surface features and probe the ugly underbelly of the creature—a perfectly normal thing for a father to do—but the important thing now was not to act so hostile that Liz got her back up. She would figure David out before long. So the thing was to be polite and friendly, make the best of the rest of the weekend, and above all, not do anything to harm his relationship with Liz.

So Ned walked out to the kitchen and told Liz and David that he was sorry if he had been a little strange that morning.

He even allowed Liz to suggest, without arguing, that he some-times "struggled" on holidays. He ended up putting a relish tray together while David was playing the role of head chef. Ned, of course, was not surprised when the dinner turned out to be excellent. The turkey was moist and flavorful, and even the stuff-ing, with all the junk in it, was not so bad. Of course, David had oversold it a little, but then, what was new about that?

*That's a better dinner than I ever cooked in my life,* Kate told Ned, and, having vowed to be kind and polite, Ned agreed with her completely.

Liz had a point too: This David really could do anything he put his mind to. And he was humble about it besides: painfully, irritatingly, "ah-shucks," cast-his-eyes-toward-the-floor humble. But Ned wasn't going to knock that. Fake humility was better than outward arrogance, he supposed.

Liz had tried her hand at baking some pies, and they hadn't turned out all that bad either. So the three went downstairs with pumpkin pie (it seemed wise to start rotating the food storage) and ice cream. David agreed to only a tiny slice of pie and a teaspoon-sized dab of ice cream, but that showed at least a touch of the human. The three watched a little football. David was wrong a couple of times on how he saw some close plays— but only wrong until instant replay proved him right. That gave Liz a chance to praise him for his remarkable eyesight.

After the game, Liz began to show the entire PBS version of *Pride and Prejudice* on DVD, which wasn't bad for the first twenty or thirty hours, but which finally put Ned to sleep again. When Liz suggested that he was snoring, Ned strongly sus-pected that she was only making that up to get rid of him, but he didn't say so. He merely wandered upstairs and dropped into bed—the most polite, most agreeable, longest Thanksgiving Day of his life, finally over.

He awoke early, and all the pent-up emotion seemed ready to break, so he slipped on his running clothes and, even though the morning was very cold, went after Snake Creek Canyon like never before. He was going to shatter all his old records, make it to the top of the pavement and maybe beyond—maybe run a mile or two up the rocky road that had scared David. But he ran a little too hard, too early, and Thanksgiving dinner was still lying heavy in his innards. By the time he hit the first tough hill, he was already panting hard, and by the time he reached his old highest mark—set a few days back, in the pre-Davidic era—he was suffering flulike pain. He did manage to struggle ahead a few more yards, but just as he turned around, he was struck by a wave of nausea that bent him almost double. He actually wanted to free himself of anything left over from *gastro boy*'s cooking, but nothing came, and he was forced to hobble home, half-sick, half-hunchback. What he never doubted for a second, of course, was that out of the dark would come the White Knight, and sure enough, there he was, loping up the road like a charger. Ned straightened up immediately, and he would have pinched his cheeks had he had time.

"Oh, Brother Stevens, have you already been to the top this morning?"

"Well, yeah. It was a little tough after eating so much yesterday, but a man's gotta do what a man's gotta do."

"I know what you mean. I guess you don't want to go back for a second climb, huh?"

"I'll take seconds on pie, but no more mountain this morning, thank you."

David liked that one. He was laughing as he galloped off

into the dark. And when he got back, after Ned had showered and tried to get his health back, David was more than generous. "I just couldn't make it to the top this morning," he admitted. "You've got to be in amazing condition, Brother . . . Ned."

Liz was up—that made three mornings in a row—and trying to figure out how a waffle iron worked. "Did you make it all the way to the top, Dad?" she asked.

Ned had a choice to make. He could admit that he hadn't, and match David's humility, or he could claim his superiority, and by doing so tell a dirty, disgusting little lie. But he didn't have much time to consider, so he chose a dirty, disgusting little half-truth. "It's not that bad, once you get used to it," he said.

> *Hey. That's not a lie. Not exactly.*
> *Of course it is.*
> *Yeah, like you never told a lie in your life.*

"I'm ashamed of myself that I gave up," David was saying. "Maybe we can run it together in the morning, and you can keep me going."

"Sure. We can do that." *I'll think of some excuse by then.*

Ned had to teach Liz how to mix up the Krusteaz mix—add water and stir—but the waffles were fine (except that David wouldn't eat them), and during breakfast everyone agreed to study all morning and early afternoon, then go Christmas shopping later on. David had never been to the Gateway in Salt Lake, and Liz thought it would be fun to go there. Then, when it got dark, they could go see the lights on Temple Square, which would be turned on that evening.

All that was fine with Ned, except that he was left alone all morning, and he felt distant from Liz. Nothing had turned out the way he had hoped this weekend, and even though much of that was his own fault and he knew it, he still resented the intrusion. But he used his time as best he could. He got his ski jacket on and slipped out onto the golf course to practice his short game: chips and pitches and putts. The way he had driven the ball the other day, if his short game had been just a little sharper, he might have stayed close to David. He vowed to work every day next spring, smoothing out his swing, but also working on bunker shots, pitch-and-roll shots, flop shots—all the arsenal of techniques that separated the good from the great. He was never going to be able to drive the ball three hundred yards, like young King David, but if Liz was still bringing him around next summer, and Ned could cut a shot here and there, learn to lag long putts more accurately, and start hitting greens a lot closer to the pin, he could maybe beat the kid on a good day. It was all a matter of will, of hard practice, of using anger as his friend.

*Just once. That's all I'd ask. Just once.*

About three o'clock, David decided that he hadn't gotten nearly enough done but was willing to take a break. Liz had already drafted her paper, and she was overjoyed. She still had Saturday to rewrite it, and she usually didn't have that luxury— since she generally wrote her papers the night before they were due. "That's great, honey," Ned said. "I've always told you, you're smart. You just need to develop better study habits. The nice thing is, since it's going to take you ten more years to graduate, you'll have plenty of time to improve yourself."

But Liz sounded defensive when she said, "I'm changing, Dad. I really am. And I've figured out how I can graduate two years from now, if I go to school next summer."

Ned liked that. Loved it. He looked at David when he said, "That's great, Liz. And I wouldn't give up on that goal—not for anything."

Ned drove the Land Rover to Salt Lake, even though David suggested that his car wouldn't use as much gas. "Of course, if we have to call AAA, that could backfire on us," Ned told him. "Those tow trucks use up a lot of fuel." The fact was, Ned could have driven his own Honda, and even thought about it, but excess had taken on a new charm for him in the last couple of days.

At least David laughed. And everything seemed pleasant in the car. Ned put his Johnny Mathis Christmas album in the CD player, and for the first time, he felt a little Christmas spirit. Kate had loved that album, and so it always carried a little pain with it, but he wasn't aching like he had last year, and one thing Ned did love was to shop for Christmas. He had never liked to tag along behind Kate while she looked for gifts for grandmas and in-laws, but he had loved to buy things for the kids, and especially for Kate. Every year, it seemed, he would hit one home run—find something for Kate that was perfect. He knew what she loved: colorful jackets and classic long skirts—stuff from Talbots. Last year he had found a gray suit for Liz that was more conservative than the clothes she normally wore, but she had looked fantastic in it, loved it, worn it to church sometimes when she came home for the weekend. Everyone told her how pretty it looked on her, especially with the French-blue blouse Ned had chosen. He had even picked out a silver pin for the lapel.

"Honey," Ned said to Liz now, "I'd appreciate it today if you'd give me some idea what kinds of things you want for Christmas. I get a big kick out of finding things for you, but I'm not sure what you need most. I can pick out a dress, or something like that, but if you need shoes or pants or a coat, let me know. Maybe you can show me some stuff you like. My taste is a little old-fashioned, I'm afraid."

"Oh, Daddy, you have wonderful taste. You always choose great things for me."

"Well, anyway, just show me the kinds of things you have in mind."

"Dad, that's something I wanted to talk to you about."

"What?" Ned glanced over at Liz. She was sitting up front with him, in the other bucket seat, and David was in the back.

"I've been thinking about Christmas this year and what we ought to buy."

"What do you mean?" Ned didn't like the sound of this. David was in the middle of the backseat, so Ned could see him in the rearview mirror. He hadn't said much since they had gotten into the car, but now Ned noticed that he was looking at Liz almost pleadingly, as though he were trying to say, "Don't get into this."

Liz sounded nervous as she began. "I had this conversation with the Markhams when they were out here last time. I really loved what they are trying to do with Christmas. It seems like something our family ought to think about."

"*Doing with* Christmas? What's that?"

"You tell him, David."

"I don't know, Liz. Every family has its own traditions. Just because we're changing what we do, that doesn't mean—"

"I know that," Liz said. "But just tell him what you're planning to do. I think it's worth thinking about."

*No, it isn't. I don't want to hear this, whatever it is.*

"Well," David said, "you know how everyone always talks about Christmas being too commercial, and how we all spend too much money? We kept saying that year after year, but we didn't do anything about it. Everyone in the family gave gifts to everyone else, and my parents were lavish in the things they would get for us kids. So last year, we just said, 'Enough is enough. Let's set some rules.' We drew names and set a price limit on the gifts. And my parents agreed to give only one modest gift to each of us."

"Well, that's certainly . . . admirable. I'm sure you—"

"But that wasn't the most important thing. It's not enough just to cut back on the presents. We decided to make Christmas a real time of service. Our whole family volunteered to work at a soup kitchen on Christmas Eve so the people who usually work there could have Christmas at home. And then, after dinner on Christmas Day, we went to an extended-care facility and sang carols for all those poor old shut-ins."

"Dad, you can't believe what great singers all the Markhams are. They sound like a trained chorus."

"Oh, I do believe it."

"But anyway," David said, "that was the best Christmas I remember. It was simple and spiritual, and family centered. I'm not saying everyone should do that; I'm just saying, for us, it was really nice."

*Don't try this, Liz. This boy turkied my Thanksgiving, but I won't let him Grinch my Christmas.*

"Don't you think that sounds great, Dad? Instead of running around wild, buying up everything in sight, we could buy one carefully thought-out gift, and with the money we save, maybe we could do something for a charity. David's too modest to mention that their family made a sizable gift to a crisis center back in Connecticut. They're also supporting several children through the Christian Children's Fund, and they do a lot of other great things with their money."

*If he's so modest about it, how did you find out?* "That's really impressive, David. No question about it."

"But what do you think, Dad? We could send e-mails to all the family tonight explaining what we have in mind—and I'll bet they would love the idea. Maybe we could ask everyone for ideas how we can make Christmas as spiritual as possible this year."

*So what am I supposed to say? I want to have another self-indulgent, overpriced, hedonistic Christmas—the kind I've always loved?* "It's something to think about, Liz. Let's talk it over a little more when we get a chance."

"Oh, yeah, I think you should," David pronounced from the backseat. "I wasn't trying to push anything off on you."

"It's not that," Liz said. "It's just a great idea. I wish it would spread everywhere—especially all through the Church."

"Maybe we could start a chain letter," Ned said.

"What?"

"Just kidding. We'll think about it. But you know, there are things you need, and Christmas just seems like a nice time to get them." He glanced in the rearview mirror at David, who was looking resplendent in a cable-knit sweater, perfectly creased gabardine slacks, and brown-on-brown saddle shoes that had probably set him back two hundred bucks. "I notice that some-one found you naked and clothed you, David. Was that in the after-Christmas sales?"

David reached the pink stage very quickly, then flushed right on through to red in another second or two. "That's a very good point, Brother Stevens. Ned. I do love clothes. And it's not something I'm proud of. I work in the summer for my father, and he pays me way too well. Then I spend too much of that money on clothing. I'm not saying that my family has overcome its materialism; I'm just saying that we made a good start by backing off on our Christmas spending."

"If everyone does that, the stock market will crash. Our whole economy is built on out-of-control Christmas spending. And think about all those little garment workers in sweatshops all over the world. If we start dressing down, they go from overworked to unemployed. I buy lots of things I don't even need—just to keep the skids greased on the good ol' world economy. I think we all need to do our part."

David was laughing, as though he rather liked that idea, but Liz sounded put out when she said, "Dad, I know you're just joking, but when half the world goes to bed hungry every night, I don't think it's a laughing matter. If we spent a few hundred dollars less on Christmas, we could feed a lot of starving people for months."

"I'm sorry. I won't eat the rest of that turkey David cooked. I'll give it to the poor."

"Yeah," David said. "Let's make sandwiches and airmail them to Guatemala."

Ned laughed and exchanged a knowing nod with David in the rearview mirror.

*You know what, Kate? There's a real jerk deep down in that boy, just longing to come out. If I work on him a while, I think I can find some layers of good old-fashioned American corruption.*

*And wouldn't you be proud of yourself?*

*A little.*

"All I'm saying, Dad," Liz said, "is that I don't want you to buy a bunch of things for me this year. I do need a coat, and if I got that, I'd be happy."

And then David—old knock-over-Goliath-on-the-way-to-glory David—grinned at the rearview mirror and said, "I think if she asks for a coat, you're supposed to give her a cloak, too."

Ned cracked up. He actually swerved out of his lane and had to get himself together just to stay on the road. David had made a joke. Not a great joke, but a nicely irreverent one. Ned almost liked him.

But Liz chastised him, and David soon repented. "I do think you're right," he told Ned. "We've maybe made a good start by improving our Christmas, but I need to change my attitude, year-round. My heart is still way too focused on the things of the world. I long to have material things, and Christ taught us, time and again, that that's the road to destruction."

*Okay. But don't take away my Christmas shopping. It's bad enough that you want my daughter.*

The Gateway was full of shops formulated upon the premise that materialism was naughty, naughty, naughty, but oh so nice. Both Liz and David found themselves a little less spiritual when they looked upon the designer shirts, leather jackets, and hand-made shoes that were normally valued only by superficial types. They kept saying, "No one needs a sweater that expensive," or, "I'd be ashamed to wear jewelry like that," but their eyes were full of dazzle, and Ned was taking mental notes. What they didn't find was much in the way of dress coats, so they decided to try the Crossroads Plaza shopping center, where Liz spotted a black cashmere coat that clearly left her weak in the knees. She decided, however, that another coat, of ordinary wool, was almost as nice, and much more "serviceable."

Ned knew what he was going to do. He would get the cashmere, and he would get the sweater she had clearly lusted after, and even the English-made shoes, plus a blouse or two, and some socks—all stuff she needed and wanted—and he would gamble. By Christmas, David could easily be the latest in a long line of former boyfriends, and Liz would be saying on Christmas morning, "Thanks so much, Dad. I'm glad you didn't listen to me. I really wanted all these things."

What ended up happening, however, was that no one was buying anything. Liz was still holding out for the Markham-style Christmas and wanted to draw names before she bought anything for anyone in her family, and David only mentioned possibilities: "This might work for my little brother. I drew his name this year." But he never decided on anything.

When Liz suggested that they all head across the street to Temple Square, Ned asked, "David, did you want to go back to the Gap and get that shirt for your brother?"

But David said, "Well, no. I've actually run out of money before I've run out of month. I'll wait until I get my check next week."

*What? Another flaw? Don't you keep your budget on a spreadsheet, or whatever it is you perfect people do?* "Hey, I can lend you a few bucks so you don't have to come back for it."

"No, I don't want to do that. I'm thinking I can get something similar, but cheaper. The BYU Bookstore has some nice clothes."

"Well, okay. Why don't you two go ahead," Ned told them. "I think I want to look around just a little more while I'm here. I'll find you over at Temple Square."

"You're going to go back and get me a coat, huh, Dad?" Liz leaned close to Ned and looked into his eyes. "I know how you work."

"Actually, I'm going to see if they have a cloak store around here." He smiled at David, and David laughed.

"How are you going to find us over there?" Liz asked. "A million people will show up at Temple Square this weekend."

"I'll just look around."

"If you don't find us," David said, "meet us at the Seagull Monument in—what?—an hour?"

"Okay. Good."

Actually, that was perfect. It was cold, and Ned didn't really want to hang around Temple Square very long. What he did want to do was head straight to the "luxury items" Liz had drooled over. It wouldn't take long. He would get the coat and a couple of other things here, and then return to the Gateway another day. He had everything staked out.

So once they were gone, he slapped his plastic down at several counters, stood in line for gift wrapping—since he was such a klutz at wrapping things himself—and dumped everything in the Land Rover. He covered the packages with a blanket he kept in the back and then hurried across to Temple Square. He barely made it in an hour, but he spotted the kids immediately, already at the monument. They were obviously cold themselves—or at least David was wrapped around Liz like Spandex.

As Ned watched, David pulled Liz close and kissed her—right there in front of the seagulls. Ned could hardly believe it. Liz just wasn't like that.

David was changing Ned's daughter; that was all there was to it. And the kid was so sneaky about it. As Ned drew close, he almost announced himself, but a better idea hit him. He slowed and tried to listen. What kinds of things did the guy say when Ned's back was turned? Did his real personality come out then, or did he stay with the Eddie Haskell routine?

But then the two began to walk away, their arms still around each other. What was going on?

Ned followed. He stayed back a few paces and watched. What was David looking for—dark shadows where he could really get it on? Had he forgotten all about meeting Ned?

The two walked east, between the temple and the South Visitors Center, where the crowd thinned out. They approached the statues of Joseph and Hyrum Smith near a little fountain that wasn't running this time of year. Ned kept his distance, but he saw them sit down on a short retaining wall near the statues. They weren't kissing, just talking, but Ned had to wonder what David might be saying. Behind them was a little thicket of shrubbery—good cover if he moved in closer. He told himself that it would be wrong to spy on them, but all the while, he was moving to the shrubs. He took a hesitant step or two off the sidewalk, stood in the snow, but couldn't hear anything, so he worked his way closer to the two. He was only about ten feet away when he heard David say something about a fifty-seven Chevy. *His* fifty-seven Chevy. Strange. Ned had never heard about that. But then Ned heard David say, in a tone of voice that was completely new—low and full of self-importance— "Yeah, I started with a rusty piece of scrap metal and I completely rebuilt the thing. It's worth a lot of bucks now."

*Oh, right. You don't brag, do you? You're the guy who invented humility—at least when you're around me.*

But Liz was saying something he couldn't quite pick up. She sounded like she had a cold. What was going on? Was she starting to come down with something?

"Dad?"

Ned looked straight up. He thought he'd heard a voice from the sky. *Which dad? Who?* But it sounded like Liz.

"What are you doing in there?"

Ned spun around. There was Liz, standing on the sidewalk.

David was next to her. Ned's head jerked back to the couple on the bench. Same black coat. Same . . . but not the same. Ned needed a shovel. He wanted to dig a hole and jump in.

But he walked toward Liz and David. "Oh, hi."

"We saw you walk over here. We couldn't figure out what you were doing."

"Oh . . . well . . . I . . ."

But now Liz was staring at the couple on the bench. He could see that she was putting things together.

"I thought I saw something blow into those bushes. I was going to get it."

"What was it?"

"I thought it was a scarf or something, but I couldn't find it. It must have blown farther away. I was just looking in the bushes . . . where I thought it went."

Ned saw David glance around, as though he were looking for some sign of wind. And he saw the perplexity still in Liz's face.

"I guess it was nothing. Are you two ready to go?"

"You haven't looked at the lights or anything yet. Do you want to see the Nativity?"

"No. That's all right. I've seen it other years. Let's just head back to the car."

"Dad, were you following those people?"

"What people?"

"Over there. The ones sitting down."

"Oh. No. I was looking for that scarf. It was a nice one. Or I thought it was. Maybe it was just some . . . paper, or something."

"Paper?"

Ned glanced at David, and he thought he saw pity in the

boy's face. "It might have been, you know . . . anything," David said. "Why don't we just go home."

And so they walked through the north gate of the square and then back across the street. Ned knew—without liking the idea—that he owed David one. But he wondered what the boy would say once he and Liz were alone. "Your dad's going off the deep end," or some such thing. Ned was still trying to get used to the idea that Liz and David weren't over on the bench talking about Chevys and having colds and getting ready to make out.

*Ned, are you wacko, or what? That guy was four inches shorter than David, and the girl's coat was blue, not black.*

*He did seem a little shorter, but—*

*But you were so ready to think the worst of him, you just couldn't resist.*

*No. No. It wasn't like that. I just really thought it was them.*

*A scarf?*

*It was the first thing I thought of.*

*I'm starting to wonder how much you lied to me.*

*No. I don't lie, usually. I just . . . felt so stupid.*

*And rightly so, my dear. And rightly so.*

# Chapter Seven

On the way back to Midway, no one mentioned Ned's little blunder at Temple Square, but Ned was feeling subdued. Liz, to her credit, seemed intent on smoothing things over. She was upbeat and talkative in the car, and when they arrived at the house, she said, "I'm in the Christmas mood now, after seeing all the lights and everything. Let's not watch another movie tonight. Let's just sit by the fire and listen to Christmas music."

Ned hoped the "we" included him. Maybe the truth was, she just wanted to cuddle up with the ghost of Christmas Presents.

David had another idea: "Why don't we sing a few carols first? Nothing helps me feel the Christmas spirit more than that."

Ned started backpedaling as fast as he could. He loved music when it came in through his ears, but nothing that came out of his own mouth could be defined as a musical note—or at least as more than one. "Maybe you two could sing a little and I'll just listen."

"No, Daddy. Let's gather around the piano for a few minutes. It'll be great."

There was a piano in Ned's family room only because it had

been Kate's. Liz had taken a few lessons as a kid, but she had decided she didn't like to practice.

*Please don't tell me he plays the piano.*

"David plays—really well, actually."

*Another big surprise.*

So they gathered around the piano—except that Ned kept turning away as much as he could while he more or less lip-synched the carols. Meanwhile, ol' golden fingers was knocking out carols without any sheet music. And he did have an *adorable* voice.

Ned was discovering something he had feared. Christmas had been terrible the year before, without Kate. He had told himself it wouldn't be so bad this year, but that wasn't what he was feeling. Kate had always played the piano at family home evenings, and with little help from Ned, she and the kids had always sounded great together, especially at Christmas. All these songs only reminded him of that, and the fact was, he was still feeling like a fool, which didn't help much. "Silent Night" was hard enough, but then David played "Still, Still, Still." Kate had always loved that song, and Liz sounded like Kate when she sang it. David and Ned let her sing alone.

Ned wasn't doing well by the time she was finished, and Liz seemed to know. She hugged him and suggested, "Maybe that's enough singing. Instead of listening to carols, we could—I don't know—play a game or something."

"No, that's fine. I'm okay." He tried to think of something to say, just to change the subject. "So, David, when did you find time to take piano lessons while you were doing . . . everything else?"

David got up from the piano bench, tucked his hands into his nice slacks, and seemed embarrassed to say, "I actually didn't take a lot of lessons. I just sort of taught myself a few things—like those Christmas carols. You've heard almost everything I know."

"David! It's a sin to lie!" Liz gave him a little punch in the stomach, then stepped from Ned to David, slipped under his arm, and grasped him around the waist. "He can play almost anything—and he does it by ear. He played in a jazz band in high school."

"When?" Ned asked. "How did you have the time? I'm sure you were also student-body president."

"No, no. I wasn't into that kind of stuff."

"You were senior class president!" Liz said, giving him a tighter squeeze. "You don't have to be ashamed of it."

David looked at Ned apologetically. "I didn't run for it. Someone put me up and . . . I just . . . I don't know . . ."

"You just won."

"Well . . . yeah."

"So what kind of jazz did you play?"

"The high school band played a lot of modern things. But I'm more into the older stuff. I like Art Tatum, Oscar Peterson—people like that—and especially, Thelonius Monk."

"You've gotta be kidding. Have you seen my CD collection upstairs? Half of it is jazz, and half of the jazz is piano stuff. I think I own everything Thelonius Monk recorded."

"Hey. All right. Let's listen to some of that. Forget the Christmas carols."

"Can you play any of Monk's material?"

"Sort of. I mess around with it a little." David sat back down at the piano. He took his time, as though he had to search for the melody, and then he began a slow, spare little tune that Ned knew immediately. "I recognize that cut," he said. He listened a few more seconds. "It's got 'Ruby' in the title."

"Ruby, My Dear."

"Yeah. That's it."

Ned couldn't believe how completely David was capturing the sound, using Monk's halting rhythm, his lean style. Ned had wished all his life that he could make music like that, and David was doing it with seeming ease. What's more, he had started with Monk's piece, but he was taking it somewhere, adding his own variations.

But then he stopped, abruptly, and turned around on the piano bench. "That's not really Monk anymore. I only remember the first part. I'm really just an imitator, not a real musician."

"Hey, don't do that," Ned said. "You don't have to put yourself down all the time. That's a gift to play like that."

"Well, thanks. My dad can't stand jazz. He never understood why I wanted to play it."

"Kate didn't like jazz either. But to me it's like the raw stuff of life—all the emotions laid bare." David nodded seriously, and the two looked into one another's eyes. Then Ned said what he was thinking: "David, is there anything you can't do?"

David smiled rather sadly. "Actually, I feel like I'm cursed. There are a whole lot of things I can do 'almost well.' Maybe I've never concentrated and given my complete devotion to any one thing, or maybe I don't have the courage to push one of my talents to its limit. It always seems to me that I've been allowed to walk right to the edge of excellence and look in—and never step inside."

Liz sat down on the bench next to David. She nestled against him again, and he put his arm around her. "You're an excellent person," she said. "It's the whole package that counts."

"If you're going to measure me by that standard, I can't even get close enough to take a peek," David said, still looking at Ned.

Ned was surprised to find that he believed in the sincerity of David's assessment, and he didn't know quite what to make of that. He tried to think of something to tell David, but couldn't. "I think I'll go upstairs and do some reading," he finally said. "You two don't need me around all the time."

Liz protested, but Ned walked up to his bedroom. He sat in his big reading chair and tried to think what was going on.

*Ned, he's not so bad after all, is he?*

*I don't know, Kate.* Ned thought for a time. *Humility is his specialty. Maybe he's developed it into an art form.*

*I don't think it's art. I think it's the real thing.*

*Maybe. But she's still too young.*

*Or maybe you are.*

*What's that supposed to mean?*

*You know exactly what I mean.*

*I'm thinking maybe he looked at my CD collection and saw how many Thelonious Monk albums I have.*

*You don't believe that.*

*It's possible. He's lied to me before.*

*And what about the scarf blowing in the wind? If I were you, I wouldn't be pointing any fingers.*

*I don't feel like talking to you right now, Kate.*

*I'm sure you don't.*

Ned told himself, one more time, that he had to stop this, but he couldn't resist saying, *I wish you could come home for Christmas.*

When Liz had been singing downstairs, Ned had remembered a Christmas in California when Kate had come home from choir practice and told Ned, "I want to move back to Utah. No matter how long we've lived here, I just can't think it's Christmas when it's so warm outside." Ned's business had been booming by then, and he was gone a lot, traveling all across the country. He saw plenty of snow in airports and busy cities, and he didn't idealize the stuff. But he told Kate he would take her back to the mountains before too many more years. The years had kept stretching, though, and the money had been too good to walk away from. Still, he might have moved his business to Utah; he could have done it if he had made the move a priority. He was just always too busy to start the process. And so she had died in southern Cal, and she had never experienced that snowy winter she wanted. Maybe, if they had actually moved, she would have hated the cold. Maybe she wouldn't have lasted a year without begging to return. But he would never know now. They had planned these years in a peaceful valley, snowed in with a warm fire, with nothing more to do than to listen to good music and read good books. And he would stay home—not be traveling all the time. It had all seemed so wonderful to Kate, and therefore, good to Ned too, but he had never kept his promise, and then he had run out of time. He felt now, especially in this new house, that he could go forward with his life if he could just have her here once, for just one Christmas.

*Ned, don't do this. You know how I romanticize everything. A snowy Christmas isn't that important. You gave me a wonderful life; you treated me like a friend and a princess, all in one. What more could a woman want? But now you have to start thinking about a future for yourself. I can't come back, and Liz is going to get married—if not to David, to someone, and if not this year, one of these first years.*

*She's going to marry David. Who wouldn't?*

*It's okay. You two can listen to jazz together.*

*Right after he takes me out on the golf course and beats my brains out—or runs me into a heart attack, up in Snake Creek Canyon.*

*You still don't like him, do you?*

*I don't know. I'm not sure I trust him. That's my little girl he wants to walk off with.*

*You took me away from my dad.*

*I know. But I was young. I didn't know what it meant. What your dad should have done is throw me out the door. I wasn't good enough for you.*

*I know. But then, who was?*

*You're not nearly as funny as you think you are.*

*And you're not as humble as you're pretending to be.*

*I mean it, Kate. You seem an angel to me now. I know I'm making you better than you were, and I keep telling myself not to do that. But I find myself wanting to come to you now, and not have to wait.*

*Ned, you don't get to decide those things, but you do get to decide how you use the life you have.*

*That's the stuff everyone says, but people don't know what it's like. I try to make things mean something to me, but nothing does, not really. Except Liz.*

*Ned, it hurts me when you say things like that. Self-pity isn't pretty. And it's not you. It's been two years. It's time to go ahead.*

*With what?*

*You know.*

*I'm not going to talk to you about that.*

And he didn't. He read instead—or tried to—and then he watched television, but didn't seem to notice what was on. He wondered what David and Liz were doing. He wished he had stayed with them and maybe played a game or worked on a puzzle, the way he and Kate had always done. But he didn't dare walk downstairs. They were creating their own little world together now. He could see it happening, and he remembered what it was like. Not long after he had started to date Kate, he had changed inside. The individuality he had protected up until then had given way and lost all meaning. He had suddenly wanted nothing so much as that two-in-oneness he had never experienced before. Every time he said good-bye to Kate, he had begun to long for the next time he would see her, even the next phone call.

All that was happening to Liz now, with David, and Ned felt as though a thief were in his house. Liz had always understood him. He had told her things he had never told his sons, and she had been willing to share whatever was in her head, to spill her emotions without precautions. She was down in the family room now, probably sharing her thoughts, her feelings, her self. Ned had worried entirely too much about the kissing. That was the least of his problems. David had her heart, and he would soon have her mind as well. And the worst part was, he probably deserved all he was getting. He was certainly a more accomplished young man than Ned had ever been.

*All right. Lay off. Kids grow up. They get married. Sometimes they even choose humble guys. Annoying guys. Perfect guys. It's not the end of the world. Maybe he'll bogey a hole someday and just break down and bawl. And maybe I'll get to be there to see it.*

Ned decided to have a go at reading again, and this time he had some moderate success.

Ned didn't get up early the next morning. He woke up, but he didn't get up. In fact, he lay in bed worrying that David would come tap-tap-tapping at his chamber door and want to go for the big run all the way to the top. *Give me a year and I'll be ready for you, mountain-goat boy.*

But he didn't hear anyone stir, and so, when the sun got up, so did Ned. He went out and poured himself a bowl of the commercial, not-really-that-good-for-you granola, and especially enjoyed the way it stuck together. By then, Ned could hear the shower running upstairs, and Liz showed up from downstairs, still earlier than Ned would have expected. She was wearing a plaid robe and had combed her hair, but she hadn't done much of anything else. She told Ned, "David's decided he'd better head back to Provo today. He's not getting enough studying done up here. I think I'm kind of a distraction for him." She said this last coyly, with fun in her eyes.

"So are you going back?" Ned asked.

"No. Not if you can drive me down Sunday evening."

"Of course I can."

"Okay. I want to stay. I've got that paper to finish today, but we do need to talk. We still haven't done that."

Ned had lost most of his interest in the subject he had originally had in mind, but he was relieved to hear that she wasn't going to leave him alone for the balance of the weekend.

When David came down, he was wearing jeans and a plaid shirt—another Polo. The kid had little horsies on everything he wore. "Did Liz tell you? I'm going back to Provo. I could come back for her on Sunday."

"No, that's fine. I'll drive her down."

David did stick around long enough to eat a bit, and then Liz walked him down to the car. Ned had lost interest in sneaking a look out the kitchen window—just to see if David kissed her good-bye. He knew the answer to that one.

But when Liz came back in the house, she said, "Come here, Dad." She walked over and switched on the gas log, and then pulled one of the chairs closer to the fire. She sat down with her feet tucked up into the chair and wrapped her robe tightly around her legs. "Let's talk."

"Do you want some hot chocolate?"

"Ooooh, yes."

Ned filled a kettle with water, set it on the stove, and fired up the gas burner. He walked to the great room and sat on the couch across from Liz. "That water will take a few minutes to heat up."

"Dad, I sent David home. I told him that you and I needed some time together."

"You didn't have to do that."

"Yes, I did. In fact, I wish I hadn't brought him. I really don't think you would have disliked him so much if you had met him some other time. You're not yourself right now."

"If you mean that I've not been very friendly to our houseguest, that might be true. But I don't know that that's any great aberration. I never have liked to have company."

"Dad, stop it, okay? You're so unhappy, I don't think you know what you're doing. What's going on? Tell me what you wanted to talk to me about."

"I don't know if I even remember."

"Dad, I know you—better than anybody does. You're struggling worse than ever, and Mom's been gone two years."

Ned was wearing a pair of khaki slacks that were worn

117

threadbare. He leaned back, stretched his legs out, and shoved his hands into those good old pockets, the fabric inside worn to smoothness. He looked up at the high ceiling. The sun was angling through the kitchen windows in front, but this room was still mostly shadowed, except that the light from the fireplace was sending off little flickers. "Okay, here's what I wanted to talk to you about. I was going to tell you that I've been struggling lately. But somehow, you guessed it."

"What's happening? Are the holidays going to be tough again?"

"Oh, Liz, I don't know. Every day is tough, and I keep thinking it's all supposed to go away."

"Do you just miss her, or—"

"Liz, I wake up in the morning, way too early, and I don't know what the day means. I don't know what anything means. So I run up that stupid mountain until I'm exhausted, and then I come home and figure out something else to do. I like the guys in the ward, and I play golf with the ones who are retired, but then they go home to their wives, and I grab at anything I can think of to fill up the rest of my time. I fish, but I don't care about fishing. I ride my bike, but I don't care about riding my bike. I'll ski this winter, but I don't care about skiing. I spend my evenings out on the deck reading, and when the sun sets or some deer show up, I catch myself saying, 'Kate, come and look.'"

"You always tell me you're doing okay."

"I talk to her, Liz. I carry on long conversations with her. I know what she would think about my life, so I have her tell me what I ought to do. And she's right. I mean, *I'm* right, but it doesn't seem to make any difference."

"Do you tell yourself you ought to get married?"

"No. That part is entirely her idea."

"Dad. That's like psychotic or something. You don't really hear her voice, do you?"

"I don't know. No. But it's still her idea. She's the one who tried to make me promise."

The kettle had begun to whistle, so Ned got up and walked to the kitchen. From behind him, Liz was saying, "You know it's the right thing to do. Didn't Elder What's-his-name tell you that?"

Ned had a good friend from his college days who was serving in the First Quorum of the Seventy. He had told Ned way last year that he needed to get married and then go serve a mission. "You'd make a great mission president," he had told Ned, "but we only send couples out to lead missions. The missionaries need a mission mom, not just a president."

Ned got the hot chocolate mix down from the cabinet. "I'll tell you what's funny," he said as he measured out the spoonfuls into a pair of cups. "Everyone has the same advice, and no one has the slightest idea how it sounds inside my head. I don't see how I can just start all over—start building again what it took me almost thirty years to build last time. You can't imagine how long it takes to know someone that well, to share a million thoughts and memories and weaknesses, until you get to the point that you aren't afraid that she's going to find you petty and stupid and disappointing—even though you know you are."

"Dad, it feels like I know David really, really well already. Some of it comes through the Spirit, doesn't it?"

Ned wasn't going to respond to that. How could a twenty-year-old understand what he was trying to say? It was all so theoretical for her. Ned hadn't known when he married Kate how many attitudes came from families, came from nowhere at all, but were part of a person, and became important only when real-life decisions had to be made.

Kate had come into their marriage thinking that the "only true furniture" was early American—or real antiques—and Ned had known just as surely that furniture like that was the ugly old stuff from his Grandma Stevens's house. The first really big argument he had had with Kate was over an ugly bedroom set she had liked: the one they had bought and Ned had eventually come to love. Within a few years after their wedding, he and Kate were spending their Saturday afternoons knocking about in dusty old antique stores. He had no idea how that had happened, but he didn't want someone with a new idea about furniture entering his life now—maybe wanting to throw out the stuff he and Kate had loved and purchased. The round oak table in their great room was one that he and Kate had found in a little shop. They had bargained hard and gotten it for six hundred dollars, had put it on layaway, and then had saved their pennies to pay it off. No one was going to tell him, "This old table is cracking. Do we really want to keep it?"

Ned poured the hot water into the cups, mixed the chocolate in, and then walked slowly to Liz, being careful not to spill. He handed her one of the cups and went back to his chair.

"Liz, a year after you get married—not that long—you'll be saying to yourself, *I thought I knew this guy*. You'll be putting your makeup on, look over, and some guy will be standing next to you shaving, and you'll think, *If I'd really known him, I'm not sure I would have married him*. And yet, if you work at it, and you love each other enough, there comes a day when you hold dear the very same things that bothered you at one time. Your mom always put things down wherever she happened to be, and then she was always wandering around looking for her purse or her glasses or her car keys. I would tell her to put her car keys in the same place all the time, the way I always did. But it's strange. I find myself leaving things all over the place now, and I honestly think it's so I can look for them and feel like—I don't know—feel like . . . I used to feel when I would help her. I think I want to find her keys sometime, or . . . I don't know. Liz, it's all such weird stuff."

"But it's great, in a way. It shows how much you love her. Someday you'll be with her again, and you'll like all the things you've missed."

"I know. And that's one reason I don't want to be made over by someone else. When I get back to Kate, I want to be the same guy. I want to pick up where we left off. It just feels like, I don't know—infidelity—to start mixing and matching with someone else."

"But no one stays the same. Twenty years alone, or thirty or forty, is going to change you more than anything. Mom wants you to be happy, and she wants your life to be full. She doesn't want you waking up every morning wondering what you're living for. You said it yourself: You can't just spend your life fishing and biking and playing golf."

"I know. So I'm stuck between a rock and a hard place, and I don't know what to do. I feel like life is getting worse the longer Kate's gone—and it was supposed to be the other way around."

"Dad, I just think you need someone in your life. Maybe you won't find anyone you want to marry, but you at least need to get acquainted with some women, go out once in a while, and see whether someone doesn't start making you feel different about all this."

Ned was sipping on his chocolate, and he almost choked

when he started to laugh. "Liz, you have no idea what you're saying. All the single women I know are after me. They're trying to cook their way into my heart. If I ask any of them out, they'll be all over me like the hair spray on their bouffant hairdos. I have to arrive at church late and sneak out early just to avoid all my groupies."

"You rock stars have it tough."

Ned grinned. "You're right about that. I'm looking for some woman who thinks I'm dumb and ugly. Her, I wouldn't mind taking out."

"Well, it'll never happen. You're just too cute."

"I know. That's my problem."

Liz was smiling, but she still looked concerned. "Dad, I love to come up here. And I love you. But I feel like you're clinging to me. And that's one reason you don't take a chance and ask someone out. I also think that's why you don't like David."

"Wow! You figured it out."

Liz pulled her legs out from under her, sat up straight, and leaned forward. "What's that supposed to mean?"

"You're stating the obvious. What do you think I mean?"

"You admit you're clinging? And you admit you have no good reason to dislike David?"

"Yes, to the first part, and 'maybe, somewhat' to the second. But I do think good old Dave deserves a certain amount of distaste all on his own."

"But why?"

"I don't want to get into all that again. Every time I say something bad about him, you like him a little better."

"But I can't see what it is you dislike. You try to tell me he's self-righteous, but I see just the opposite. He's trying so hard to be righteous that he's too self-conscious about it, but that's

122

not such a terrible thing. He just wants to do what he's supposed to do—and to live up to what everyone expects of him."

Ned wondered about that. He had seen some of what Liz was talking about. He set his cup down on the end table next to him and folded his arms. "I could be wrong about David," he said. "I admit that. But he comes in such pretty gift wrapping, I'd advise you to wait until you see what's inside before you start committing yourself. That's all I'm saying. Give it time. Don't let him talk you into getting married right away when you've still got so much life ahead of you."

"Is that the clinging part of you talking now?"

"Yes. But it's also the guy, more than any other in this world, who doesn't want to see you make a mistake."

"Okay. So I have your advice, and you have mine. I say, 'Go slow, but find someone. I think you'll be happier with someone in your life.' And you're telling me, 'Go slow, but find someone. And be careful about this David dude before you let him into your life.'"

"Yeah. That's about it."

"Okay, and I say, 'I love you, Dad, even more than David—and more than anyone in this world'—and now, let's go roller-blading."

"Oh." Ned sat up straight. "Okay."

The truth was, Ned had a secret talent. He had been a pretty serious roller skater in his youth, and he knew some tricks. He had converted his talent to roller blades in recent years but felt like an idiot skating out on the streets of Midway. Liz was the only person around anymore who knew that he could skate backwards, do three-turns and mohawks, and even throw in a flip jump—single, not double—or a loop jump, when he was feeling brave. Right now Ned was more than happy to drop all this seriousness and just have some fun with Liz before she left again.

So they got on their coats and walked down to the garage, where Ned was able to dig out their roller blades from the closet that contained all his fishing and skiing gear. (His golf stuff filled a whole bedroom, which he was going to have to clear out before the rest of the family came home for Christmas.) The street in front of the house was relatively smooth and rarely busy, and therefore a good place to skate. They could roll down the hill toward the Blue Boar Inn, pick up some serious speed, then loop in a circle through the housing development, back around to the house. Ned had been trying to teach Liz to skate backwards for years, but she would start to pick up a little skill and then not skate again for months. Today, they circled the neighborhood forwards a couple of times, as much as anything to stay warm, and then Ned did start getting a little fancy. He did a few turns and then glided backwards in front of Liz. "Come on, try it," he kept saying.

"Show me again. I don't know how to turn when I'm moving."

Ned did some fancy three-turns, forward and then back again, but Liz said, "Not that way. I can't do those. Show me that two-footed turn you do."

So Ned lifted all his weight to his right foot, turned his body, and let the heel of his left skate come down behind his right heel. Then he simply let the weight shift from right to left as his body continued to turn. It was easy. "Ta-da!" he said.

But when Liz tried, she didn't have the confidence to turn far enough with her weight on one foot. Catapulting herself into something of a spin, she ended up doing a full three-sixty instead of a one-eighty, and was completely stopped.

Ned stopped and skated back. He laughed at Liz's funny, low laugh, and then said, "What you did was this." He pushed off forward and tried to imitate her awkward turn, but he exaggerated a little. His right foot flipped off its edge, and suddenly he was airborne. He turned in the air and managed to land on his seat, not his side, but he hit pretty hard. He was stunned for a moment, and then he looked up at Liz, whose face was full of concern—as though he had just fallen off a cliff. He laughed, even though he was in a little more pain than he wanted to admit.

That set her off, and she stood over him, laughing, making that barking sound of hers. He loved the way she looked, so delighted, so bright, her eyes so round and blue against her dark hair. She really was beautiful.

When Liz put out her hand, Ned pretended that he wanted the help, but instead, he pulled her down. She might have landed rather badly herself, except that he caught her, and they ended up sitting next to each other on the cold blacktop, and Liz was smacking him across the shoulder. "You did that on purpose," she said.

"No way. I'm an elderly man. It's hard for us old people to get up." But then he popped up quickly and pulled her up.

"You're the superstar of roller-blading, Dad. I'll never be as good as you."

"I couldn't agree more. I may join the roller-blade follies and travel throughout the world, doing axel jumps and camel spins."

"You can't even do those."

"That's true. But I'll work hard, and never give up."

Liz had seen something. She was looking toward the vacant lot next to Ned's house, and her eyes had gotten big. Ned turned to look. A small doe and a fawn were standing near the top of the lot. The two had apparently jumped the white vinyl fence that ran along the golf course, probably intending to cross to the creek in the valley below. But they had stopped now and were both staring at Ned and Liz, standing stiff, their ears straight in the air, their eyes big.

"Oh, they're beautiful," Liz said, but they were not thirty yards away, and the sound of her voice seemed to set them off. The doe spun and bounded away. On her third leap, she cleared the fence and then trotted off across the golf course. The fawn followed, except that it hopped to the fence and stopped. The poor thing must have jumped the fence before, but it had lost confidence this time, maybe because it was now on lower ground. It stared at the fence as though it had no idea what to do, but the mother was still trotting away.

The fawn took another step toward the fence and then chose an easier way. Instead of jumping over all three rungs, it took a kind of dive over the second rung and under the third. But that was awkward, and the little fawn caught its hind legs halfway through. Flailing and scrambling, it fought its way through and finally sprawled on the other side. It was up instantly and chasing after its mother in that wonderful leaping motion that looked jaunty and poetic for the doe, but bouncy and funny for the fawn.

Ned and Liz were both laughing just to have seen the fawn lose its dignity and find it again. Then Liz said, "Sometimes that's what you have to do, Dad—whatever you can manage for the moment. You know. Just make your way over—or through—that next fence, whether you look graceful at it or not."

Ned thought about that. What he wished was that he knew

what fence he needed to jump. He had never been afraid of challenges he could see—just the ones he couldn't define.

He put his arm around Liz's shoulders. "But don't trot off like that mother, okay? I still need you around for a little while." She looked up at him, and he saw that she had taken his words seriously. He knew it was something he shouldn't have said. So he added, "Besides, I need to teach you a few more things before you go out and face the cruel world on your own. A girl is really not ready for life until she can roller-blade backwards."

That could have been funny, except that Liz had begun to cry.

# Chapter Eight

Ned's next week was not as bad as he had feared it would be. After he took Liz back to Provo, he had a serious talk with himself—not with Kate. He had no reason to feel sorry for himself. He had a good life—one he had dreamed of during those hard years when he was working way too many hours. He was reaping the benefit of his labor, and now it made sense that he take a little time to relax.

Ned did do a little more checking on David, and he learned some things that disturbed him. He had actually begun to feel better about David that last night he was in Ned's home, but the things Ned was learning had now convinced him that his first impression had not been wrong. The lie about the wedding reception was not the only one David had told. Still, Ned decided not to call Liz. Right now, if he said anything, she would accuse him of meddling and being suspicious. He figured it was better to let her find out for herself. If she didn't get the picture pretty soon, he would definitely have another talk with her—but only as a last resort. He wasn't the kind of father to meddle or to tell his adult children what to do. His own dad had been a little too free with his advice, and Ned had never liked that.

Ned decided he had to concentrate on the future and make

choices that would get him in the right frame of mind. One of these days he would get involved in a new business, or he would decide to take a trip around the world, or . . . something—there were all kinds of things he wanted to do. Golf was over for the season, and he wasn't one to fish all winter the way some guys did, but there wasn't any snow yet, so he could still run the canyon, or bike, if he felt more like doing that.

Plus he had started a new project: He had begun to make a list of "books I've always intended to read." He owned at least a hundred books he had never gotten around to, and in addition, he drove to the Barnes and Noble and the Deseret Book in Orem, found another twenty or so books he wanted to read, and bought about half of them. So he now had an exciting collection of material, and he saw the winter ahead as "the year I finally get educated." In college he had majored in business but had always found history and literature and psychology more interesting. He had gone through life always feeling jealous of the Ph.D. types in the wards he had lived in. He was going to study the scriptures as never before, with lots of reference and background books, and he was going to read some of the great works on world history and American history. And for fun, he would mix in the classic authors: Milton, Dickens, Tolstoy, Dostoyevsky, and the best of the Americans—Melville, Twain, Faulkner, Hemingway.

He had become excited as he studied bibliographies of great works, listed the names, located the titles he already owned and those he needed to purchase. But halfway through the first chapter of *The Rise and Fall of the Roman Empire,* his enthusiasm waned just a bit, and his mind wandered at times. He got in a good bike ride and then came back for more, telling himself that he would gradually get used to spending more hours reading than exercising. He would savor a kind of Walden Pond winter, cozy inside his house while the snows fell outside.

By Wednesday, Ned had discovered the secret to success. Reading the same book all day was a little too numbing. The trick was to read one chapter at a time out of several books, and to mix in a thriller or a murder mystery, just for a change. And by the end of the week he hit on an even better idea: every Friday would be his "light-reading day"; he would allow himself his favorite indulgence, Louis L'Amour. He also came up with an important innovation for Saturday: "sports on television day," just to give his mind a rest.

So it wasn't a bad week. Ned had tried to think as little as possible about Liz, and especially David, although he caught himself wondering every evening whether they were together. Liz called almost every day, but Ned and she were both careful not to talk about subjects that were "awkward." One thing Ned did do was put in a lot of time preparing his Sunday School lesson. He was "loaded for bear" when he walked into the church, with way more information in his notes than he would ever have time to get to. In his preoccupation, however, he made a crucial mistake. He mistimed his driving time and arrived three minutes before sacrament meeting would start, and there in the hall was Carol Holly walking toward him.

Carol was new in the ward and she was divorced. Ned knew that much about her. She was certainly pretty—tall, with a slender figure and longish, reddish hair. (Although Ned figured the red tint came from a bottle.) She had one of those knockout smiles you could see from a hundred yards away, but that was the problem. It was overstated. There wasn't a hint of slyness in it. It seemed to say, "Here I am; to see me is to know me." That was all well enough, but she always beamed that smile in his direction with more enthusiasm than he trusted, and besides, Ned had seen enough toothy smiles lately to last him for a while.

Now she was walking toward him, moving fast, teeth blazing, hair flowing like something out of a shampoo commercial. "Ned!" she announced, way too loudly, as though she were trying to call all the single women in the ward down upon him.

Ned felt like saying, "You don't know me well enough to shout my name like that," but instead he only said, "Hi." He refused to say her name.

She broke off her charge, even though it had seemed so purposeful just a moment before, and stopped in front of him. "How was your Thanksgiving?" she asked. "Did Liz make it home?"

Ned was surprised that she remembered Liz's name. Liz had been at church with Ned a couple of times that fall, and Carol had met her, but Ned certainly hadn't memorized the names of any of Carol's kids—some of whom also showed up from time to time.

"Yes. In fact, she came to church with me last Sunday."

"Oh, I was gone. I spent the holiday with my daughter in Las Vegas. My son from California was there too, with his family. We had a great time."

"That's nice."

"Didn't you say you have all your kids coming home for Christmas?"

How did she remember stuff like that? He had no idea what her plans were, and yet, he was sure he had "made conversation" with her on the subject some week not so long ago. "Yes. Everyone's coming."

"Even your son from Belgium?"

"Wow. You have a good memory."

She shrugged, but her smile enlarged, even though Ned hadn't thought that possible.

"But yes, they are coming. In fact, he'll be here for two weeks, with his wife and three kids. I hope next year they can come for *one* week."

Carol laughed knowingly and patted his arm. (She had that move, too.) "But that's great," she said. "I've decided to stay home. My kids all want their own Christmases, at home, and I could go to one of their houses, but I don't know, I love Midway. I'd kind of like to get snowed in. You know, just hunker down by the fireplace with a good book and have a little quiet time. My business is so busy just before Christmas that I'm ready to put my feet up by then."

What was the woman doing with her eyes? If she had said, "Neddy, boy, why don't you slip over and keep me company some evening?" she couldn't have been more obvious.

Ned felt himself flush for no good reason, and he said the only thing that came into his head. "That's what I've been doing lately. I'm on a big reading project. I'm trying to read some of the 'great books' that I've never read."

"Wow. That sounds wonderful. Are you working from a list or just choosing things as you go?"

"I've put together my own list."

"Isn't that funny? I've got a list too, but I don't get to it all that often." Ned knew that she commuted to Salt Lake. Her business was one of those boutique things: gifts or crafts or something of that sort. "We ought to exchange lists some time. It would be interesting to see how many of the same titles we have."

"Yeah. Let's do that." The woman was becoming a little more obvious all the time. Ned started working his way past her.

But she didn't move. She leaned toward him just as Ned tried to get by. Her nose was almost touching his. "Sorry to scare you, Ned. We certainly wouldn't want to get our lists all entangled."

"No. I . . . uh . . . I'll bring mine to church next week. I don't mind."

"Or maybe I could bring mine over on a tray, with a casserole. But I hear, so far, no one has had much success with that technique."

Ned was dumbfounded. He couldn't believe she would say something like that. The woman was cocky, for one thing. She knew how pretty she was, and she thought she could disarm him with all this straightforward flirtatiousness. He only smiled, or maybe ducked his head. He wasn't sure what he had done, but he was soon flying down the hall toward the chapel, afraid that she might follow.

It was not one of those Sundays, like the week before, when hundreds of visitors from all the condos and second homes in the ward had made the meeting look like a stake conference. Ned managed to find a seat in the chapel (as opposed to a folding chair in the cultural hall, where he ended up most weeks). By the time he sat down, he was realizing how embarrassed he was. He hadn't needed to flee the woman. He could have played it cool, exchanged the banter, and then walked away with a little dignity. But what did he care? So what if she thought he was a doofus? It certainly didn't matter to him whether he impressed her or not.

*I think she's really funny, Ned. And smart.*
*Don't you think she's a little obvious?*
*Sure. That's what I like.*
*Of course. It's the kind of thing you would have done.*

*I didn't say it. You did. And don't worry about being such a doofus. You always were, and I fell for you.*
*Who's worried? I'm not worried.*

But he vowed, next time Carol teased him like that, he was going to be aloof with her, let her know that he wasn't some sixteen-year-old boy, flustered by a pretty girl.

It was fast and testimony meeting, but Ned could hardly keep his mind on what the various members said during their testimonies. His mind kept going back to the little encounter in the hallway. Hadn't that word *entangled* been just a bit suggestive? He did pay attention when Sister Riley, another single woman in the ward, mentioned that she had not given up on the idea that the Lord had someone for her. He had no problem with that, but he wondered why, every time he looked up, she seemed to be staring straight at him. What bothered him more was that Carol had chosen a pew off to his left and a little in front of him. He could see her whenever he glanced her way. That, too, would have been all right, except that twice—once wouldn't have been so bad—she looked toward him and caught him looking at her. Even that wouldn't have been terrible if she hadn't smiled the second time. It made him furious that she was finding some significance in the mere fact that his eyes, in scanning the room, had happened to pass in her direction.

He also found himself struggling to concentrate during his Sunday School lesson. Carol didn't smile at him, but she paid careful attention, as though she didn't want to miss a word. And yet, his words were anything but memorable. He kept getting mixed up in his notes or turning to the wrong scripture. That was the problem with overpreparation, he decided. He needed to keep his next lesson focused on the essentials, not on . . . other things.

Ned was glad when he could retire to his high priest group and just listen to the fellows argue about whether God's foreknowledge could be reconciled with the determinism implied by that knowledge. As it turned out, it could be; everyone agreed on that. They simply didn't know how. At least nothing was new. Brother Tucker, a member of the group, did drop a bomb—as he did almost every week. God knew all things, from beginning to end, he said, and if a reader understood certain coded language in the book of Revelation—and in particular references in the Dead Sea Scrolls and the writings of Nostradamus—he could determine the year of the Second Coming. According to Brother Tucker's own calculation, it would probably happen in 2011, although he was willing to admit that he might be off a year either way. Ned was glad that the group arose almost in chorus and told Brother Tucker that "no man knows the day of His coming." Tucker only smiled knowingly and nudged Brother Rittlesbacher, who also smiled—which proved that he had only *appeared* to be asleep.

Ned had served for a time as a high priest group leader, and he had been in a couple of bishoprics before he had served as a bishop. All those years in those callings had taught him to be patient with eccentricities. Mormons came in various shapes and sizes, he had learned, especially among converts. He always knew when he heard what people said in church that there was a story behind those opinions, those ways of doing things. One thing about the older high priests—they were comfortable with their beliefs, and a man could say almost anything in the meetings without worrying the others too much.

Ned said not a word, enjoying the whole thing. These were good brothers. But as he left the group, and thought of going back to his empty house, he felt the return of some of his sadness from the week before. He could put in another day of reading, but what he really wished was that Liz had come home. It would have been nice to nuke something for Sunday dinner, share it with her, and then have someone to talk with during the quiet hours of Sunday afternoon. He had his music, his books, his fireplace—and even some predicted showers of snow—but he was going to have that stuff all week, and he longed for some life in his house today.

But he caught himself. He picked up his pace and vowed he would make the day a nice one. He wasn't going to feel sorry for himself. He decided he would sneak out the side door and then loop around to the back of the building where he had parked. He tried to vary his pattern from one week to the next so that no one could lie in wait for him. Sister Riley, after her proclamation, was certainly "in the mood for love," and needed to be avoided at all cost. Ned could almost guarantee that he would get at least one dinner delivered today, and probably cookies, a pie, maybe some Rice Krispie treats—or all of the above. Some Sundays he picked up enough food to feed him all week. That wasn't all bad, of course, except that the fresh things he bought often spoiled before he got to them, and of course, returning the dishes still frightened him more than anything he ever had to do.

He was almost to the side door of the church when he heard someone call his name. He was startled for a moment until he realized that he was hearing a masculine voice. He turned around to see Bishop Nelson. "Ned, do you have just a minute?" he asked.

Bishop Leonard Nelson—Len—was a savvy guy, and likable. The role of bishop came naturally to him. He understood the love part, so all the other stuff fell into place. But he also had more advice for Ned than Ned had ever asked for. Ned sometimes tried to avoid him, too. But now he found himself saying, "Sure, Bishop. Time is one thing I've got plenty of."

He walked with the bishop back to his office. Bishop Nelson closed the door and motioned for Ned to sit down, then walked around his desk. Ned hoped he wasn't getting a new calling. However much he had messed up the lesson today, teaching Gospel Doctrine was still his favorite Church job.

"I had a strange phone call from a bishop this week," Bishop Nelson said. He was a man with less face than seemed normal for such a good-sized head—as though what little he possessed had had to be stretched. It left him with lots of cheek space but a narrow little nose and a skimpy mouth. "I was wondering whether you knew anything about it."

*Oh . . . nooooooo.* "I'm not sure what you mean, Bishop."

"I got a call from a BYU bishop. He said that someone had called him, asking for information about one of the students in his ward. This man wanted all sorts of worthiness information, and yet he had no logical reason to explain why he needed it. He identified himself as Bishop Nelson from Midway, Utah."

Ned knew he was in trouble, but he wasn't going to roll over easy. Bishop Nelson was going to have to work for this.

"*I'm* Bishop Nelson, Ned."

"Yes, you are."

"And I didn't call him."

Ned was nodding, but still not coughing anything up.

"Ned, the bishop had caller ID."

*Busted.*

"And the caller ID I-Deed one Mr. Edmund Stevens. Unless I'm mistaken, *you* are Edmund—a.k.a. Ned—Stevens. And if that weren't enough to make one wonder, coincidentally, this

'Bishop Nelson'—the one with your caller ID name—also happened to have your phone number. That seemed a little odd to me."

*A bishop should never be sarcastic.* "I confess."

"What's going on, Ned? I think it's a federal offense to impersonate a bishop. You may end up doing hard time."

Ned had made the call on Monday, knew the BYU bishop hadn't bought his story, and had felt like an idiot ever since. The thought of caller ID had crossed his mind, but he had allowed himself to hope that he couldn't be that unlucky.

Obviously he could be.

He could also be humiliated. That's what he was now. "I wasn't trying to do anything underhanded. I was just doing some research—some very, very important research."

"Is that why you asked the bishop whether David Markham had any honor code violations against him? And by the way, who is David Markham?"

Ned took a long draw of bishop's office air. He decided to wrap the whole thing in a small package and then hope for forgiveness and escape. "Bishop, my daughter is dating the Markham boy. I have reason to suspect that he isn't all he ought to be, and out of love for my daughter, I wanted to learn what I could about the boy—and protect her, if necessary. It was wrong to claim I was you, but I was afraid I would only get the usual platitudes if I identified myself. This Markham kid puts on a very good show."

"Ned, your daughter is in the same ward. The bishop sort of put two and two together. He had a pretty good idea what was going on. He called me mainly because he wondered whether you were going into some sort of psychotic break."

"I was only looking out for my daughter."

Bishop Nelson folded his arms, then used them to prop himself up as he leaned over his desk. "This Bishop Rawson, I think his name was, told me that David Markham is the most impressive young man he's met in his years serving at BYU."

"That doesn't surprise me one bit."

"So what are you so worried about?"

"Have you ever met a young man who has all the right answers when you give him your bishop's interview, but something still tells you not to trust him?"

"Yes, I have."

"Or sometimes you meet someone who seems to throw off glitter when he smiles, and he knows all the right things to do, to say, to claim—and yet, you have this feeling that what you see is not what you get?"

"Yes. I've felt that too. But now let me ask you a question."

"All right."

"Have you ever met a father who thought no young man, no matter how noble and worthy, was good enough for his daughter?"

"Yes." Ned found himself slipping lower in his chair. "But a father has the right to inspiration for his family, and if he feels this really creepy feeling about a guy his daughter is dating, he has a right to . . . take action."

"And the best course of action is usually to claim he's a bishop, even if he isn't, and make calls under an assumed name—specifically my name?"

"No. But when you feel like your child is in danger, maybe you resort to methods you wouldn't normally use." Ned liked that. And the bishop was nodding. Ned was finally getting himself up off the floor after the initial knockdown.

"Well, okay," Bishop Nelson said. He was still leaning on his elbows, still looking thoughtful. "Let me first suggest that you not use this particular method again, no matter how protective you're feeling. We don't need fake bishops running around the Church. We may have to start excommunicating a few—just to make an example of them."

*I liked you a lot better before you decided to be so clever.* "Look, I'm sorry. I knew it was the wrong thing to do. I just couldn't think of any other way to get the information."

"Let me suggest, secondly, that you do some careful thinking and praying about the source of these negative vibes you're getting about Brother Markham."

"What's that supposed to mean?" Ned sat up straight.

"I know what Liz means to you right now, Ned. And I understand that completely. But don't scare a good young man away just because you don't want Liz to get married yet."

"Why not? She's way too young to get married."

"Isn't she about finished with college?"

"No. Not at all. She keeps changing her major. She may not graduate for another decade, the way she's going."

"Isn't she twenty-one or—"

"No. She's twenty."

"She must be close to twenty-one."

"'Close to' and 'is' are two different things."

"True. But I'm just saying, she may be a little on the young side to be getting married, but a lot of Mormon girls marry before they finish college. It's one of the best times to meet a young man—and most of them keep going to school these days, and the two both finish. The time to get married is probably when you meet the right person, not when you reach any particular age."

"Maybe so. But that's why I want to find out whether he is the right person."

"Isn't that *her* job?"

"Liz changes her mind about what she wants to wear five times before she gets dressed. And this guy is dazzling her right now with all his big, white teeth."

Bishop Nelson smiled just a little and shook his head. "But Ned, if she is sticking with him—and not changing her mind—that ought to say something to you."

Ned realized he had mixed his arguments. He knew he had to recover quickly. "She's easily influenced. That's all I'm saying."

The bishop was thinking again. Ned started to slide forward on his chair. Escape time was coming. "I'm just wondering why Bishop Rawson liked the boy so much, and you find him so offensive."

"Because David Markham is on the offense. He's got more moves than a point guard—and quicker hands."

"What do you mean? Did you catch them doing something?"

"Yes." Ned knew he was in trouble. He wasn't going to answer the next question. He had been down that road before.

"Something serious?"

"Not exactly. But it was in my house, and they haven't been dating that long."

"Something morally—"

"Bishop, I don't think a girl should kiss every guy who takes her out. A kiss is serious. Kids these days think it's just—"

"That's what they were doing? Kissing?"

"No. But almost."

Now the bishop was staring at Ned with that "are you all right?" look. Ned was getting tired of that. "Almost?"

"He lies, Len. I caught him in a bald-faced, blatant lie."

"What did he lie about?"

"He wanted to get Liz alone, so he told me—and made Liz say the same thing—that they were going to a wedding reception. I could tell they were making up the whole story. And Liz has never been like that. He's changing her."

"Do you know for sure they were lying?"

"Yes. I called the reception center. There was no reception for anyone named Johnson that night. It's an open-and-shut case."

"Did you ask Liz about it?"

"Not yet. But I will."

The bishop finally leaned back in his chair. Ned had picked himself up off the mat and had landed a solid blow. He wasn't looking quite so crazy now. "Ned, I can see why that might trouble you. But sometimes people do things for innocent reasons. Maybe they wanted to do some Christmas shopping for you, or . . . who knows what? To tell you the truth, what worries me almost as much as the lie you think they told you—"

"*Did* tell me."

"Well, yes. But what worries me is that you called down there. If you thought Liz was lying, you should have asked her. Frankly, this so-called research you're doing sounds just a little nuts."

*Ugh. Counterpunch.* "I wouldn't have done it if I hadn't had suspicions. All kinds of stuff has been going on. David told me he wasn't much of a golfer, and then he went out and knocked the cover off the ball—just to humiliate me in front of my daughter. And he likes this little game where he pretends he's all humble and meek, and never brags, and then he lets you know somehow that he can do just about anything. He turns out to be a star athlete, an A student, a jazz musician, a General Authority's kid, a—"

"He's a General Authority's son?"

"One of those Area Authority Seventies. Not an apostle."

"But that ought to be a pretty good credential."

"Not when he uses it as some sneaky little thing he doesn't tell you himself, and you have to find it out from someone else."

Now the bishop was getting that, "this is worse than I thought" look. Ned hadn't wanted to use it, but he decided to pull out his big blow. "He lies about all kinds of things—even when he doesn't need to. He told me he was friends with Brig Jenson, the congressman. And I found out it isn't true."

"How did you find out?"

Ned didn't want to get into that, so he said, "We were watching TV after Thanksgiving dinner, and Jenson was on the news. So I told him that the congressman was a friend of mine—which he is. So David says, 'He's a nice guy, isn't he?' like he thinks he's really cool and knows everybody. So I asked him, 'Do you know Brig?' and he said yes, he had had dinner with him one time, although he couldn't come up with an explanation for why that would have happened."

"But maybe it was true."

"No way. I don't buy it."

"He may have been invited to some sort of event at the Y, or—"

Now Ned had no choice. He had to say it. "I called Brig and put the question to him, and Brig said he had never heard of the guy."

"You called the congressman about that?"

"Yes. And I'm glad I did. The evidence just keeps piling up."

"Maybe the Markham boy did meet him. The congressman might have forgotten. Those guys go to all kinds of dinners."

"But David was talking about what a nice guy he was, like they were buddies. I think Brig would remember if they got to know each other that well."

"Did he say they were 'buddies'?"

"Well . . . not in so many words."

"Did he say it or didn't he?"

"That's what he implied. It's what he wanted me to believe, that's for sure." Ned stood up. It was time to stop talking. "So anyway, Bishop, I'm sorry about that phone call I made. I won't do anything like that again."

"Ned, are you going to be all right? What if Liz does decide to marry this fellow? Are you going to go off the deep end on me?"

"Not me. I'm fine. David's not a terrible guy. Maybe she can bring the best out of him. So if she chooses him, she chooses him, and I'll just have to accept it. But you can't blame me for trying to help her, now that I know how much he lies."

"Ned, I think it's great for a father to counsel with his daughter, but I don't know about all these calls you're putting in. It sounds to me like you're desperate. And I think that has more to do with losing your wife than it does with Liz. I know you're lonely, and loneliness does things to a person."

Ned headed for the door. "I'm over all that, Bishop. I've got two years behind me now, and I'm doing fine."

"Hold on just a second." Ned had hold of the doorknob, but he did wait. "I've told you before that I really think it's time for you to meet someone, to date a little. When I met Carol

Holly, my first thought was, *she'd be perfect for Ned Stevens.* Have you gotten to know her at all?"

Ned gave that one some thought—or pretended to. "I think I know who she is," he said. "But Bishop, I'm sorry; I've got to go. Thanks for all the help."

And Ned was gone. He loved the bishop; he really did. But now the man was starting to sound like everyone else.

# Chapter Nine

Ned was a little upset when he left the bishop's office. He was a lot more upset by the time he got home. The more he thought about it, the more it bothered him that no one seemed to trust his instincts. Liz claimed she would be careful before she committed herself to David, but the girl had lost all objectivity. She was in love; she couldn't think straight. And Kate was still standing over Ned's shoulder telling him how "cute" the boy was. She was as bad as her daughter. Now the bishop was giving Ned lectures about "going overboard." Never mind that Ned was only trying to be a good father.

Ned kept telling himself that he needed to let things run their course and not say anything more to Liz. But it was Sunday afternoon and the house felt hollow as a cave. What would it be like when Liz was on the East Coast and there was no one to come home, no weekend visits to look forward to? And then a memory struck him, and it did him in: He had come home from a business trip, back when Liz was maybe ten or eleven, and she had been sitting on the front porch, waiting. She walked around to the garage as Ned pulled the car in. "We need to talk," she said as he stepped out of the car, and then she took him to her room and shut the door. "Dad, do you think it's all right for me to go with a boy?" she asked.

"Go with one? Where?" he asked her.

"No. Not go someplace. You know. *Go* with him. Mom says I can't."

"Well, if Mom—"

"But she calls it dating, and we won't go on dates. It's just going together."

"You mean he likes you and you like him. Right?"

"Well . . . yeah."

"Did he write you a note or something?"

"Dad! No way. We're not in second grade."

"So how did he ask you?"

"He had his friend ask my friend."

"Oh. Okay. Got it." And then Ned pretended to think the whole thing over, very carefully. Finally, he told her, "I think it's okay to go with him as long as you don't go anywhere."

She had grinned with those teeth that still looked a little too big for her face. He could still see those huge blue eyes and her Dutch-cut hair—so much like the haircut she had now. "Thanks, Dad," she had said. "Don't tell Mom, but I'd rather talk to you about things. You don't get so emotional."

But after, when she had run to call her friend—not the boy, but her girlfriend—Ned had wondered whether he had said the right thing. He didn't want boys to start liking her. He wanted her to be that great kid she was forever. Since then she had liked lots of boys, and even more had liked her, but she had always kept some of that kid quality. It just seemed wrong for her to give all that up. She wasn't really grown up; Ned knew that better than anyone. David was the sort of guy who would take her and mold her, make her over into an entirely different person.

Ned was already beginning to have a change of heart—thinking that he'd better intervene now, after all—when something happened that clinched it for him. The phone rang and it was Ned's friend Oscar McPherson on the line. Oscar was a guidance counselor at BYU. "Yeah, Ned," he said, "I got your message about the Markham boy that you wanted to hire. I'm sorry I didn't get back to you, but I've been out of town all week."

"Oh, that's all right. But can you tell me anything?"

"I can't release a transcript to you until the student requests it."

"But did you look him up?"

"Yes, I did. He's a great student. Have him fill out a release and then I'll send you the information you asked for."

"Okay. But I need to make a decision right away."

"I thought you had retired, Ned. What are you doing, starting a new business?"

It flashed through Ned's mind that he had just finished repenting in the bishop's office, and this was no time to start making up new stories, but he didn't have a lot of time to think, so he said, "Yes, I'm looking to start a new one."

*"Looking to start" is not the same as "starting," and I'm always considering possibilities. Maybe the bishop would call that a lie, but it's actually more or less true in a kind of general way. And I do have a job open, after a manner of speaking. I may not have announced an opening, but Liz did, apparently.*

"Can you at least tell me this?" Ned asked. "Does he have a perfect four-point-oh?"

"I'm not supposed to—"

"Oh, come on, Oscar. You can tell me that much."

"Well, no. It wasn't a four-oh."

"Then he lied to me."

"I wouldn't say that, Ned. I mean, it was very close to a four-oh. Three-nine-eight, or something like that."

"But if he said he never had a grade other than an A, he would be lying. Right?"

"He could have had some A-minuses."

"But he didn't say anything about A-minuses."

"Look, why don't you just get him to release the transcript, and then you can look it over. He's obviously a first-rate student. His grades are almost perfect."

"So, Oscar, would you say that there's a difference between 'almost perfect' and 'perfect'?"

"Of course, but—"

"So if a guy claims to have a perfect GPA, and he's got only an almost-perfect GPA, he's a small liar—not a big liar, but he's still a liar. Right?"

"So what are you saying, Ned? You'll only hire a guy who's perfect?"

"I just want him to be perfect when it comes to lying and not lying. The job I have open requires more than a fairly good guy."

Ned got off the phone after that, even though Oscar was still arguing that an A-minus here and there wasn't a big deal. Ned was surrounded by people who couldn't see the difference between right and wrong. It said something about what was happening to the world, in all its corruption. But the important thing now was to plan a strategy. He had promised himself not to interfere in Liz's life, but the girl was about to fall off a cliff. What kind of father was he if he wouldn't reach out a hand to her?

He stood in the kitchen and stared out across the valley for a few minutes, and suddenly he knew. He was tired of strategies.

It was time for a caring father to do what he had to do. He hadn't wanted to say anything to her, but what choice did he have now? He had changed his clothes and was wearing his tired old khakis and a sweatshirt, but he didn't bother to get dressed up again. He didn't even put a belt on. He just grabbed a coat—his ski parka—and headed down to the garage. This was going to be the day he reasserted some order in his family. Liz had to be set straight.

He drove faster than he normally would, even though he wasn't sure that Liz would be home. Ned's block of meetings hadn't ended until two, and her meetings were earlier, so she might be off with friends—or with David. But Ned was ready for that. He would just have to stake out the house, and when David came walking in with her, probably expecting a smooch at the door on a Sabbath afternoon, Ned would be there to shout, "Stop right there, *pucker boy.* I've got the story on you now." Then he would report the newest of David's lies and watch him slink off with his tail between his legs.

Someday—maybe not today, but someday—Liz was going to thank her dad for this. When David ended up in jail for embezzlement or theft by deception—or whatever it was he would finally do to show his true colors—Liz would say, "Thanks so much, Dad, for protecting me from my own silly choices. I lacked your maturity and discernment, but I was too young to know that at the time. Thanks to you, I waited a few years to marry, and now I have a wonderful husband, beautiful children, and a happy life. I might have experienced a life of misery, wed to a man who deceived me from the beginning, but it was you, my dear, dear father, who led me away from the precipice I had approached and was gazing into, not understanding how deep and dangerous it really was, and not knowing that David was trying to shove me over the side when I thought, all along, he was a fine guy. But you knew. You knew. And you saved me. And for that I will . . ."

*Okay. Okay. I know. Liz doesn't talk like that. But she* will *thank me.*

*Ned, I know you're not going to listen to me at this point, but just let me whisper one little idea in your ear.*

*Go ahead.*

*You're talking about an A-minus. Maybe two. Three, at most.*

*That's the trouble with people these days, but I wouldn't think you—living where you do—would accept that kind of morality. Since we can't expect people to be* completely *honest, we'll settle for* fairly *honest? Is that what you're telling me? Well, I don't happen to buy into that kind of morality.*

*Wait. What's that before my eyes? I see a scarf blowing in the wind.*

*I repented for that. And it was a completely different thing. I was trying to save my daughter. All David's lies are attempts to lead her astray.*

*Wait again. Is that you, "looking to start" a business?*

*In a certain sense, I am, Kate. And I have no evil purpose behind my . . . choice of words.*

*Ned, listen to me. You're making a big mistake.*

*Get off my shoulder. I'm on a mission.*

*This is going to be a bad scene, Ned. I think you know that already.*

*A man's got to do what a man's got to do.*

When Ned arrived at the apartment, he was glad to see Liz's little Neon parked out front, and even happier to see no pile of

Corolla junk parked anywhere nearby. And when he rapped on the apartment door, he was overjoyed to see Liz open it. She had changed into jeans and a T-shirt, so there was no sign she was going anywhere, and when she smiled—with obvious joy at seeing her dad—Ned was sure he had done the right thing.

"I need to talk to you, honey." He stepped inside. "Are your roommates around?"

"Heather is in her bedroom."

"Okay. Well . . ." He wasn't sure how to do this. "There's something I need to tell you, and I'll speak softly, so Heather won't hear me."

But just then the bedroom door opened and Heather stepped out. "Oh, hi, Brother Stevens," she said.

"Hi. Hey, listen, do you have anything you could do in your own room for a minute? I need to talk privately to Liz."

"Actually, I'm just leaving. Sit down and take all the time you need."

Heather got her coat from the closet by the door, said good-bye, and left. The way was being opened for Ned. This was definitely a good omen. He felt some of the tension leave his body, and now he had to stay calm, speak with authority and yet with tenderness, and make sure that Liz understood that some things, no matter how difficult, were for the best.

"Go ahead. Sit down," Liz said, but she was looking concerned now. Ned sat on the little sofa—or *love seat* might be the accurate term, considering what probably went on there. Liz sat down next to him. "Are you upset?" she asked. "You seem kind of nervous."

"No, no. I've never felt better. But I told you I was going to keep doing some checking, and I've done that. It's not easy to tell you this, Liz. I know you really like David, and I know

152

he seems to be a great guy—if you don't know the whole story—but there are things going on here that don't add up, and you know, when a guy claims to be perfect, he invites scrutiny, so anything I've done I've done for you—and none of it is really wrong if you're doing it to protect your only daughter against an unhappy future and a lot of grief while her husband is doing jail time or . . ."

*Settle down. Take a breath.*

"Jail time?"

"Well, you know, not necessarily. I'm just saying, one lie leads to another, and things can go that way. Every criminal starts out probably lying to his mother about the cookie he took from the jar, and then he's taking a few pennies from her purse, and eventually dope usually gets involved before . . ."

*Hey. Hey. You're losing it. Talk straight. Tell her what you know.*

"Dad, what in the world are you talking about?"

"Okay. Let me just lay it all out. David is not what he seems. I've got proof now. First off, he lied to me about that wedding reception, and he made you lie about it too. It never happened. I don't blame you, because I know it was his idea, but you kids were lying to me."

"I know. We did lie, but it's something I can explain."

"See, that's just the point, Liz. First, he had you lie, and then he says that it's okay—for this reason or that reason—but see, the reason doesn't matter. He's either a man you can trust or he's one you can't trust, and he's either pulling you down to his level or he isn't. It's all these relative values that are getting us into trouble. I'm not going to let him drag you by the hair, kicking and screaming, down into the mire of lies and deceit."

"Just let me tell you what we were doing that night."

153

"It doesn't matter what you were doing. Don't think I'm going to start accepting situational values."

"Dad, David got a call that afternoon when we were out on the golf course. He—"

"Is this your explanation for the lies?"

"Yes. I guess you could call it that. But—"

"I don't want to get into that right now. If you have moral issues, you may need to talk to your bishop, and then—"

"Dad! I have no moral issues."

"So lying's not a moral issue? Is that what David has been trying to tell you? That's exactly the logic I would expect from him."

"No, no, no. *Listen* to me."

"Not yet. Let me lay it all out, and then you'll know why I'm here." But Liz looked angry. She slumped back on the couch and crossed her arms. He had to be gentler. "Honey, I love you, and I know this is hard, but it's better to know now, not after you've married the guy."

"Just tell me what you've got to say, Dad."

*Uh-oh. She really is angry.*

"Okay. I'll just take the tape off with one big pull. It will pull some hairs out that way, but the pain is over a lot faster."

She rolled her eyes, but she didn't say anything.

"Okay. I'm sorry. I'm going to put it to you straight and simple. Remember that night we were watching the news and David said he knew Brig Jenson, the congressman?"

"Yes."

"Well, I called Brig. And Brig's never heard of David."

"He just said he met him."

"He made a specific comment about Brig being a great guy. That was clearly designed to give the impression they were on friendly terms. But Brig told me that he never in his entire life has ever heard of, spoken to, or become acquainted with a boy named David Markham."

Liz twisted in her seat and looked into her father's eyes. "Dad, come on. This is unfair. All he said was that he sat at a table with him during dinner, and that the congressman was nice. I'm sure a congressman meets lots of people, and it would be easy enough to forget."

"But when the lies keep stacking up, a red flag should go up."

"What lies?"

"There are more. I've just begun."

Now Liz did look concerned, and Ned had the feeling he had turned the corner. His research was paying off.

"What did you tell me about David's grades?"

"That he's had all A's. It was his sister who told me that. But then David told us about that B he got in junior high."

"But he never corrected you otherwise, did he? He left us to believe that, other than that one B in shop, he had had all A's, all the way through school."

"Yes."

"I checked on his GPA, Liz, and it paints a very different picture."

"Are you serious?"

All Ned had done was worth it, just for this moment. She was staring at him, looking alarmed and worried. She would soon be crying about her disappointment and hugging him. He was sorry to hurt her this way, but he would help her through the dark days ahead.

"Yes, honey. I'm serious. If he had all A's, he'd have a four-point-oh, and the truth is, he doesn't."

"Was it really bad, or—"

"Let's not get into all those relative values again. A lie is a lie."

But skepticism was showing up in those intense blue eyes again. "What *was* his GPA?"

"Actually, I'm not supposed to say. Technically, I shouldn't be given that information, but I have a friend who has access to student transcripts."

"So who's the one with the relative values?"

"Liz, that's not fair. I did this checking for you—to help you avoid a fate worse than death."

"What was his GPA, Dad? If you can tell me what it wasn't, you can tell me what it was."

*I can't tell her. She's going to miss the whole point if I tell her.* "Liz, he claimed to have a perfect GPA, and he doesn't have one. There's no use talking about how big the lie was."

"He wouldn't necessarily have a four-oh. He could have some A-minuses."

*Tell me she didn't just say that.*

Liz twisted now, took hold of Ned's arm and gripped rather hard, as though she were thinking her next move might be to choke him. "Dad, tell me the truth. Was his grade point really high—close to perfect?"

Ned needed to think, and she wasn't giving him time. "What concerns me, Liz, is that you're making excuses for him now. Instead of looking reality straight on, you're hedging about the fine points. I've proved him to be a liar, and now you want to know how big of a liar he is."

"Dad, tell me what his GPA was. If you're going to accuse him, then give me the facts."

*Stall. Think of something.* "I've never said that David isn't smart. I'm sure he's a very good student. What I'm talking about is a tendency he has to slip across the line and let us believe things about him that he knows very well are not true."

"I've never seen him do that at all. You're the one playing with the truth, if you ask me. I want to know what his GPA was, and you don't dare tell me." She was gripping tighter.

*Ned, just tell her.*

*It's opening Pandora's box, Kate. It will confuse the whole point.*

*No. It's the truth, and you're the guy extolling honesty.*

Ned leaned back. He didn't look at Liz when he said, "He had excellent grades. Mostly A's, but—"

"What was it?"

"I don't know exactly. But it was above three-point-nine."

"That means A-minuses, Dad. His sister must have meant that. She said he had all A's, but she was including A-minuses."

"So the sister tells the first little white lie, and then David goes along with it. I don't see the difference."

"It's not a lie. If I told you I got all B's, that could mean B's, B-pluses, and B-minuses. What you've done is prove that David's sister was right, and David is honest. He's the one who corrected his sister and told us about the B in junior high. It sounds to me like he's meticulously honest."

*Throw a saddle on your horse, cowboy. You've just been run out of town.*

*Not yet. I'm still—*

"Dad, you're the one who lied." She let go of him and slid away. "You were trying to spy on us that day on Temple Square, and you said you were only looking for a scarf. And you're

157

breaking every rule in the book, calling people for information they aren't supposed to give out, and checking with your congressman buddy, just to see if you can catch David on any little thing he happens to say."

*It's time to skedaddle, research boy. The sheriff's got her six-guns out.*

"Anything I've done, I've done for you."

"No, Dad. I'm sorry. But it's for you. And I don't want any more of it. I want you to leave me alone. I know you're going through a hard time, but you're doing things that are wrong. I don't trust you anymore." She stood up, as if to dismiss him.

Ned felt as though a trapdoor were opening and he was about to be dropped into a black hole. If he walked out the door, he could lose Liz forever. David would have her all to himself. So he stood his ground—or actually sat on it—but he couldn't think what to say.

When things can get worse, they usually do—or so it seemed to Ned. Right then the doorbell rang, and when Liz opened the door, there he was. The Beloved. He stepped into the apartment like he was accustomed to entering that door just as he pleased. Then he pulled back his lips and showed all those piano keys. "Hey, Brother Stevens. How are you? Good to see you." He crossed the room in three giant steps, without so much as a "Mother, may I?" and shook Ned's limp hand. Then he looked at Liz. "Our a cappella group just got back from the retirement home where we were singing. It was so great."

Enough was enough. "What a cappella group?" Ned demanded to know.

"Oh, it's the one—"

"Name the retirement home. If I called the place right now, would they verify you were there?"

"What?"

"Daddy!"

"You heard me. Is that where you really were, or is this just one more of your lies?"

David was staring at Ned.

Liz said, "Dad, please. Just go home. This is all out of hand now. You need to do some hard thinking. I don't even want to see you until you get yourself together and start acting like a normal human being."

Just then Ned heard the music. Angels? For a moment, he thought it was a CD playing somewhere, but he realized the sound was coming from outside. Someone—a group of people—was singing in harmony, "Far, Far Away on Judea's Plains."

David looked at Liz. "That's our group. We're heading over to the hospital. I thought you might want to go with us."

*Neddy, there really is a group. And I'm sure there really was a retirement home. In case you haven't noticed, you just hit bottom.*

"Fine," Ned said. "You two go to the hospital and sing. And David, while you're there, maybe you could stop by the lab and do a little work. If you could find a cure for cancer this afternoon, everyone would be very thankful to you. It's the only thing left that you haven't done."

Ned walked out. He tried to look dignified, indignant, above the fray. But all those sweet little a cappella boys were singing in his face and smiling like keyboards.

Ned felt numb by the time he got home. He was humiliated,

of course, but what hurt him even more was the thought that he may have estranged himself from Liz forever. When he walked upstairs from the garage, he couldn't think what to do. He hadn't bothered to eat and still wasn't really hungry, but he decided cooking would occupy a little time. Then he realized that he'd better check outside his front door first. When he did, he found a dish of enchiladas, ready to be heated; a plate of pumpkin cookies with chocolate chips; and a bag of vanilla popcorn. The enchiladas were labeled for convenience, and the goodies included little envelopes, but he didn't check out the sources of his wealth; he merely popped the enchiladas in the microwave. He ate, tried not to think, and then looked at the newspaper, but he didn't care what was in it, so he put it down and walked out to the deck.

It was cold out and starting to get dark. He watched until he saw the first stars appear. By then he was shivering, but he stood there anyway. He felt empty, and he kept staring at the sky, wondering where heaven was.

*I wish you weren't just me talking. I wish you could tell me where you are and what it's like. Right now, I feel like I want to be where you are.*

*Ned, you shouldn't talk that way.*

*I know. But don't tell me tonight. And don't tell me how stupid I am. I figured that one out for myself.*

*Liz will forgive you.*

*Maybe. But I've lost her now. She's going to marry him.*

*Explain that one to me, Ned. How is that "losing her"?*

*He'll change her. He's going to take away all her spontaneity. She'll be as dull as he is in a few years.*

*That sounds like some of the reservations my dad had*

*about you. Remember that time he told me to "think twice" before I made my decision.*

*Yeah, well, that doesn't prove anything. Your dad was right. If you had married that Merkle guy, or whatever his name was, you would have been better off. He made a million bucks by the time he was twenty-five.*

*I know. But he had thin lips.*

*Lips? Sometimes, Kate, I think you're way too superficial.*

Ned heard that laugh he loved so much—like Liz's. He decided he'd better stop doing this. He needed to go inside. He needed to figure out something to do this week—something besides trying to read all day. That just wasn't working. Maybe he could brainstorm some business ideas. That was what he really needed, to get back to work.

But he couldn't resist a last comment.

*I still think he lied about some things. You can all tell me they're not big lies, but it's enough to raise some questions. It's not like I'm entirely nuts.*

*Just a little nuts?*

*Yeah. A little.*

*I don't know, Ned. I think, if you got the whole story, those lies, as you call them, would explain themselves away. And let me make one last comment, since you did.*

*No. I don't want to talk about . . . what you want to talk about.*

*You saw it coming, didn't you?*

*Well, yeah. You can't say a word without me thinking it up. So don't start acting like you're way ahead of me.*

*You still need to think about Carol Holly. You know that, Ned.*

Ned watched the fading light over the mountain. A glow from the Salt Lake City lights always appeared at this time of the evening. He usually liked the reminder that all that busyness and traffic was down there, not up here in the valley, but tonight this deck—and all the open space behind the house—seemed a little too remote.

*I like Carol, Ned. She understands the game, but she doesn't want to play it. She knows that you're interested in her; that's why she teases you.*

*She's too showy, Kate. She grins too much.*

*She looks great, and she seems open. I think it would be exciting for you to get to know her.*

*I don't want to know someone else. I don't have the patience or the energy.*

*Oh, come on, Ned. You're not old enough to talk like that. Remember how much fun it was when we were getting to know each other? It's exciting. It's invigorating. It's exactly what you need.*

*I remember that time we talked all night—on a Friday night—went home and slept for a while and then went for a picnic on Saturday afternoon. Do you remember that? We were just getting to know each other and we couldn't get enough.*

*It was an amazing time, Ned. I know. I was a kid, really, and I don't think I had anything very important to say, but you wanted every bit of me, starting with anything I had in my head. I hadn't known that anyone could love me that way.*

*That's what I don't think I could ever create again— or feel again.*

*But you can. Just treat her the same way. Talk to her; listen to her. If you don't have anything to say to each other, you'll know it right away.*

*I'm not sure I even like her.*

*Maybe you won't. But you're also thinking, maybe you do like her. So you need to find out. You two could travel together. Or start a business together. Who knows what? But you need to start thinking about the future.*

*Kate, I don't want to forget the past. I don't want to forget you.*

*You don't have to forget me, but you can't spend your life walking backwards. One of these days I'm going to take a hard line and just stop talking to you. We did agree to that, you know. Many times.*

*I know.*

He stood for a while longer, willed himself not to say another word to her, and then he walked back into the house. Stopping in the great room, he had the feeling he might stand there forever because he couldn't think of a single thing he wanted to do. But the phone rang. He let it ring twice while he tried to decide whether he would answer; then he walked on into his office, stood close to the answering machine, and let it pick up the call. "Dad, if you're there, pick up, okay?"

So he did. "Hi, Liz."

"Dad, I'm sorry."

"Not as sorry as I am."

"David and I had a long talk this afternoon. We decided we're not going to date anymore—not for now, at least."

Ned felt sick. "Honey, all I said was, you ought to be careful before you make up your mind."

"I know. But David feels like it's not fair for us to do something that's hurting you so much. You've been through enough these last couple of years."

"David feels that way?"

"I do too. But he's the one who talked me out of my anger. He said that there are certain steps to overcoming grief, and you're still not finished with them. You don't need to feel like you're losing me, too."

*Oh, brother. Now the kid is compassionate and self-sacrificing. How am I supposed to compete with that?*

"He cried, Dad. He does want to marry me. He just thinks we need to wait until the time is right. I need to look after you for right now."

"Liz, you don't have to look after me. Just go ahead and make up your own mind. I'll stay out of it."

"Dad, I can't keep going with him if it's going to make you so unhappy. How could I ever marry him if you dislike him so much?"

"Liz, it's been done before—lots of times." There was a long silence during which Ned hated himself. So he added, "No. I'll be okay with the whole thing. It's my problem, not his."

"Do you mean that?"

"Not yet, but I will before long." He tried to laugh. "I'll work on my attitude."

"I don't think this is funny, Dad."

"I know. It's not. You just do what your heart and your spirit tell you to do and I'll follow your lead."

"I love you, Dad."

"I know. It took a lot for you to call me tonight. I appreciate it."

"It was David who—"

"Yeah, you mentioned that."

And now everything was tense again. So Ned said, "I love you, Liz. Just give me some time to get my head on straight. Then we'll talk again."

"Okay. I'll come up."

"No. Don't do that."

"Don't you want to talk to me?"

"Sure. But not right now."

Liz was quiet for a long time, and then she said, "Okay. I guess you'll just have to let me know when you're ready."

"Sure. I'll do that."

# Chapter Ten

Ned went to bed early Sunday evening, but that only meant that he awakened early on Monday. He lay in bed for a time and reviewed his stupidity. He really couldn't think of one thing he had handled right lately. The fact was, David was going to be his son-in-law whether Ned liked it or not; he had to start getting used to that. It could be worse. There was no question that the boy had a lot going for him. But what was all that business about breaking up for dear ol' dad's sake? Did Liz really buy all that? Even the tears? Ned didn't have a chance against a guy who knew how to cry at all the right times.

Ned thought of taking his run, just to get himself up and going, but it was cold, and the thought of trudging up that mountain made his stomach sick. He tried to roll over and go back to sleep, but that didn't work, so he got up and ate his granola at the corner of the long dining room table. The sun wasn't up yet, and a long day was looming. Ned had no idea what to do with his time. He would do some reading, he supposed, and maybe go for his run in the afternoon when the temperature was a little higher. For now, he walked down the front steps and was relieved to find that the newspaper was there. That was something.

Ned took his time with the paper, and then he showered and

dressed. By then, he was thinking that maybe he should get out of the house, not read, but he was still trying to come up with something to do when the phone rang.

Ned walked into his bedroom and picked up the phone. He suspected that only Liz would call this early, and yet he hoped it wasn't her. He had no idea what to say to her at this point. "Hey, Ned, are you up?"

Ned knew only one voice that rough and hollow—like the inside of a cement mixer. It was his friend Brig Jenson. "What do you mean, 'up'? I've already put in half a day of work."

"Yeah, right. And people say that politicians tell the biggest lies. You're a lazy bum and you might as well admit it."

This morning the accusation sounded a little too much like the truth. Ned only laughed, and then he said, "So what's up, Brig?"

"*I* am. And I'm already at the airport, about to get on a plane back to Washington. But I got thinking about that Markham boy you asked me about, and I think maybe I remember who he was. Is he from back east?"

"Yes. Connecticut."

"I think his father is some big corporate executive."

"And the Area Authority Seventy back there."

"Oh, is that right? I didn't know that. But here's what I remember. I think that's the boy I gave an award to. He worked out here one summer, the way I remember it. He was a guide for a company that takes groups down the Colorado River on rafts. Some kids were sunning themselves without their life jackets on when they hit a bad stretch of rapids and their boat turned over. This boy I gave the award to was in another boat, but he dove in several times and got everyone out—three people, I think, maybe four. We gave him one of those presidential citations for bravery."

"Yes. That would be David."

"Heck of a nice kid. You could tell he was embarrassed to stand up there and get the award, but then he gave a little speech that was downright eloquent. I was thinking I ought to hire the guy for my staff. He could write my speeches."

"Yup. He would be good at it."

"And my wife. I've never seen her like that. She was all twitterpated. She couldn't quit talking about him. He's a good-looking son of a gun."

"Yes, he is. And Brig, I really appreciate your calling back. You've told me just what I needed to know."

"Do you know what the boy's plans are now?"

"I think he wants to marry my daughter, go to med school, and then run for public office. King of the World, or something of that sort."

"Well, he's going to go far. You're a lucky man."

"I suppose. I guess I shouldn't feel bad that my daughter is way too young to get married. A man needs to sell when he can get the most cows."

"How old is she?"

"She's twenty, but she—"

"Oh, come on. What are you fussing about? I married Gwen right out of high school—before she got any uppity ideas that she was my equal." He laughed, making a sound like rolling rocks. "Of course, she figured that out later. Now I'm trying to convince her that I'm her equal."

"Okay, Brig. Well, it's been good talking to you."

"Listen, this little lady here is saying I gotta get on this plane, but are you okay, Ned? You don't sound like yourself. Do you think you retired a little too early?"

"Maybe so. I'm starting to think so. But thanks for calling. Don't consort with any known Democrats."

Brig laughed like a landslide again and said good-bye.

Ned was left sitting in the chair by his bed, but he felt as though he might slide out. His backbone was turning to rubber. At least he knew the truth. David did know Brig Jenson, and not only that, he had saved a whole riverful of innocent teenagers from certain death. And just to make things a little better, he had kept the secret in his own little heart. Ned had been trying to take on Superman in a fistfight; no wonder he was all bruised up.

So Ned was finished with his "research." The only thing left was to figure out why he was the only person in the world who didn't feel a warm glow whenever David walked into the room. He didn't want to think about that now. That mountain, with all its pain, suddenly looked like an inviting diversion. So he started over, pulled off his clothes, and got his sweats on.

*That's the spirit, Ned. Quit whining, and go after life the way you always have before. A good run is just what you need.*

*Hey, you and I aren't talking. Remember?*

*I know. I'm just happy to see you stop moping around.*

*Great. I'll see you later.*

*But I do have one thought I wanted to share.*

*I'm not interested.*

*I think you bring out the worst in David. He knows you don't like him, so he's always under pressure around you. That's half the problem between the two of you.*

*I don't see that at all. He's Mr. Smooth with me, the*

*same as he is with everyone. I just see through him better than most people do. But then, you're always going to over-rate him. You're a woman, and women can't resist those big eyes and those long eyelashes.*

*Don't forget his build. His muscle-to-fat ratio must be like—*

*That's enough. Okay?*

*Oh, come on. He is gorgeous, but that doesn't mean that I—*

*You're out of here.*

*But—*

*You heard me. I'm going for my run, and I'm going all the way to the top this time.*

Ned headed for the door, and he didn't even stop to stretch. He set out with gruesome determination, pushing hard and long. He made it farther up the mountain than ever before: two-thirds of the way to the top, at least. It was only when his legs actually began to buckle and he was beginning to feel dizzy with pain that he admitted to himself that he wasn't quite ready to make the full ascent. But when he turned back, he knew he would make it a little farther every day. He would run in snow and ice, and he would drive himself ever harder until he could skip up that mountain like a kid going off to kindergarten, and he would one day run the mountain with David and talk about humility all the way, maybe even teach him a thing or two. In fact, that was a good project. Ned would study humility, every aspect of it, read every scripture and General Authority talk on the subject, become one of the world's great humility experts, and then instruct David in detail. He would show David who knew the scriptures, who could answer gospel questions, and at the same time, teach him a thing or two he needed to know.

*What good does it do to study humility if you're just going to turn it into—*
*Hush!*

Ned was wiped out by the time he got back, but that was good. He was moving ahead with his life, not licking his wounds. Liz could have David if she wanted him. He was probably better than most guys she might pick. His only flaw was a cloying, super-sweet, holier-than-thou, pious, preachy, sanctimonious, and smug self-satisfaction. Surely Ned could learn to live with that, maybe even love him for his overzealousness and his inflated self-esteem, even gradually enjoy his shy revelations that he had solved the problem of world hunger, brought peace to the Middle East, and stopped picking his nose. Perfection, after all, wasn't a fault—even if having it as a houseguest could be tedious. Besides, Ned could probably corrupt David's kids, teach them to cuss and to take Mulligans when they golfed.

Ned showered again, got dressed again, and then went after *The Rise and Fall of the Roman Empire* with renewed dedication. That was something else he was going to do: learn something about everything. When Liz brought David home next time, Ned would dazzle the guy with ready information, amazing facts, and intriguing insights.

But after two hours of "rise," with no "fall" in sight, Ned was feeling some of the same weariness he had felt on the mountain. So he drove into Heber City for an early lunch. He wanted a half-pound hamburger with onion rings, but he had his "build" to think about, so he settled for one of those Subway sandwiches that helped that guy on TV lose all that weight. As he ate, he decided to get online and look for a good deal on some weight-lifting equipment. Running was one thing, but he needed to think about flexibility and upper body strength too.

That might even help him drive a golf ball a few yards longer. He wondered whether it would be too cold that afternoon to work a little more on his short game. This was all good, what was happening to him. He was getting his fire back.

*Ned, I thought the run was a good idea, but I'm not sure what you're trying to prove with all this other stuff. Weight-lifting equipment? What's that about?*

*Health.*

*You're tall and slender. You look great. I wasn't trying to say that you needed to bulk up your shoulder muscles. You're fifty-three years old. You're never going to look like a college kid again. And you don't need to.*

*I'm not listening to you. Talk all you want.*

*I'm just going to say two more words.*

*Say whatever you want. I'm paying no attention.* Ned began to hum "The Battle Hymn of the Republic," rather loudly.

*Two words: "Carol" and "Holly."*

*Hey, thanks. That's a good reminder. I do need to start thinking about Christmas. I'll go buy some Christmas cards now, and this afternoon I may find time to compose a Christmas letter.*

*You need to think about her, Ned.*

"No," he said out loud. He wasn't going to think about her—or any other woman. That whole issue had nothing to do with Ned's present situation. What he needed to do was deal with his new reality. He had to accept the fact that some guy, even if it didn't turn out to be David, was soon going to run off with his daughter. And the other truth was, Liz would probably never find a husband who satisfied Ned entirely. Of course, it would be nice if she could find a guy who played really bad golf, but no one she met would have all the right qualities. Maybe David would be hard to take at family gatherings, what with all Ned's sons and daughters-in-law being such inveterate smart mouths, but David could resort to crying, if nothing else worked, and that might actually be quite effective—at least with the women. Besides, humility discussions were always nice, and David could lead out on those.

*Ned, don't do that. I can't believe how unfair you're being. That isn't like you.*
*Do you think I don't know that?*
*Well then, do the right thing. And you know what that is.*

Ned did know, but he waited until late afternoon before he did it. Then he had to leave a message on Liz's answering machine and wait for her to call back. When she called, Ned spoke humbly. He knew how to do that now. "Liz, I'm sorry about the things I've said to you. Especially yesterday. You're right. I've been acting really stupid. David is a fine young man, and I've been wrong to say such negative things about him."

"Dad, I understand. And I'm sorry I got so mad at you. I really think I should come home this weekend, and we could try to talk things out."

"Would David be coming, or—"

"No. We're not going out for now. I told you that."

*Say it, Ned. Right now.*

"Liz, I don't want that. Call him up and tell him that's not necessary."

"I think I'll wait until after you and I talk. I'm still not sure that you could handle it if David and I were to commit to each other."

Ned took in a lot of breath. "Sure, I can. David's a wonderful boy. I'm the one with the problem."

"Dad, I want to tell you why we lied to you. I think that might help you feel better about everything."

Ned gripped the phone hard. He was sitting on his bed, a couple of pillows tucked behind him, and trying to mellow out. But the thought of giving up the one last suspicion he was harboring was almost more than he could stand. "Sure, honey. Go ahead and say whatever you want."

"I know it was a lie, Dad, but it was mostly a cover-up. There was something David had to do, and he didn't want you to know."

"Why not?" Ned really didn't want to hear this. These stories all had the same ending.

"While we were playing golf, David got a call from the director of the homeless shelter in Provo."

"Okay. I gotcha. Enough said."

"The thing was, David volunteers down there two nights a week, but so many people were out of town during the holiday, the manager was short of workers."

"Yup. I figured it would be something like that. I understand completely."

"But Dad, he just felt like he couldn't tell you. You were already hinting that he was some sort of goody-two-shoes, and he didn't want to make a big deal of himself. Do you know what I mean? He didn't want to sound all noble and tell you, 'I must go do my duty to the sick and afflicted.'"

"I see what you mean. I understand completely."

"You don't sound like it."

"No. I do mean it. I think you've met the guy you're going to marry. And I don't think there's a better young man anywhere. You have my blessing." *Ned!* "Really. You do. He's a good young man. I doubt you could ever do better."

"But you don't like him."

Ned was willing to capitulate, but he wasn't quite ready to claim a lot of love for the boy. So he said what he could. "Honey, if I don't like him, it's my problem, not his. I mean that. I've just got some things I've got to work through."

"So do you want me to come up this weekend?"

"Uh . . . no. I want you to go out with David and make sure everything's okay between you two. I'd hate myself if he started dating someone else while you two were not seeing each other."

"Are you sure?"

"Yes, I am. I need to figure out what I'm going to do with my life, and I don't think you can help me on that one. I've been way too dependent on you since your mother died. I've got to figure out how to enjoy my life when you're off with David at medical school."

"It's not for sure yet, Dad."

"Well, then, you better reel that big fish in. There are a lot of other girls with hooks in the water."

"Oh, man, that's true. If I'm not careful the girls in my ward are going to sell me into Egypt or some such thing. Every time I look at them, I see murder in their hearts."

"Then I'd write up a contract and get David's name on the line. There's nothing more frightening than a love-starved BYU coed."

"Dad, that's not nice." But she was laughing. "Do you really think I should go ahead and say yes, if he asks?"

Now it was Ned who was hesitating. But he told her, "Do

what you feel is right, honey. Don't let my temporary insanity become part of the equation. I'm about to start looking for the cure."

"What does that mean?"

"Nothing. I'm just being metaphorical. You know, it's one of those 'physician, heal thyself' things."

"Or maybe—"

"Don't finish that sentence."

But Ned did know the end to the sentence, and it had been drifting in and out of his mind all day. Of course, with Kate still hanging around, it was a thought that was hard to escape.

Still, it took him until seven o'clock to work up the nerve, or to think he had, and nine before he actually made the phone call. And when she answered the phone, with that full smile in her voice, he almost lost his power of speech. It was only the thought of caller ID that kept him from hanging up. "Hi, Carol?"

"Is this Ned Stevens?"

"You must have caller ID."

"Well, true. But I've been having premonitions."

Ned couldn't believe it. She had no right to start jumping to conclusions. He tried to sound entirely businesslike as he ignored her words and said, "I was sitting here tonight—you know, by myself—and I was thinking that someone ought to start a family home evening group for the single people in the ward."

"It's interesting you would call. I'm home alone tonight too, and I actually thought of calling you, but I didn't dare. You're scared of me as it is. I was worried that if I called, I'd frighten you off forever."

*Why does she always say things like that?* "Well, anyway, it just seems like a good idea. Some of us could get together and maybe figure out a curriculum, and you know, have some refreshments, or . . . whatever."

"Soooo . . . what do the others think about it?"

The question wasn't all that insolent, but the little laugh in her voice was. Ned thought about cutting her with some cold remark and then getting off the phone, but instead he stammered, which was the most embarrassing thing he could have done. "Well . . . uh . . . uh." Finally he said, "Actually, I haven't talked to all that many, so far."

She was laughing for no reason he could understand, and then she said, "Ned, by any chance, did you call me first?"

But that made him laugh too—in spite of himself. "Actually, you were the last person on my list. I just happened to pick it up upside down."

"Was it hard to read that way?"

"It might be for some people, but I have the remarkable capacity to turn words over in my mind. They often spin around in my mouth too—as you may have noticed."

"So tell me, Ned. Do you like me?"

"What?" Ned had started to think this was going to be fun. But she bowled him over with that one.

"I like you, Ned. Do you like me?"

"What is this, elementary school?"

"No, it isn't. But I'm at a place in my life where I've lost interest in subtlety and indirectness. Do you really want to start a family home evening group?"

Ned took a breath. "No. I hate those things."

"So do I. Did you want to form a study group with just me then?"

"I'm not sure. I think I was going to form a group, if you

177

liked the idea, and then watch you for a while, and if you didn't turn out to be really stupid, or really boring, or—"

"You would ask me out?"

"I guess. But I was trying not to think too far ahead. This whole thing scares me to death."

"So I was right about that part. But let me suggest a possible problem. If you invite all the single women in the ward over to your house, along with the three widowers, all of whom are over seventy-five, you would create a scene right out of WrestleMania. Those women would be clawing each other just to sit next to you."

"Oh, come on. It's not that bad."

"Who feeds you, Ned?"

"I feed myself."

"Then why do you carry dishes to church every week?"

"So I won't have to go to their houses."

They both laughed, and Ned felt little electric charges inside his head, his chest. It was like a leg waking up after it had been numb.

"So do you think we ought to skip that part?" she asked. "We could just go out once, and then if I turned out to be stupid or boring—or you did—at least you wouldn't have all the others to deal with."

"Actually, that makes a lot of sense."

"Ned, I talked to your daughter one time. She told me about Kate. I don't think I'm much like her."

"I know."

"I have some experience with this stuff, my friend. Sometimes a guy, after he loses his wife, thinks he has to find her again. I tried to force myself to be what a man wanted one time, but I won't do that again."

"That makes sense. But you *are* like Kate in one way. You're straightforward, maybe even more than she was."

"I haven't always been that way. But I'm fifty—in case you're wondering—and I've gotten myself into a few situations I later regretted. I don't want that again. I was married to a man who lived in his own fantasy world. I put up with it for quite a few years, and then he had a fantasy that a twenty-eight-year-old girl would make him happier than I did. So he left me. That was eight years ago. Trust me, it's not bragging to tell you that a whole line of guys have worked me into their fantasies since then. But the dating game has been the worst trial of my life. So if I tend to cut to the chase, you can understand why."

"I just wanted to take you out for dinner or something. I'm still at that stage where this thing that everyone has started calling 'a relationship' makes me quiver."

"Then don't ask me out. I really don't want to go to dinner and a movie for five years, only to find out that you never intend to marry again."

Ned tried to talk. He couldn't. The silence seemed to go on for a week, but she didn't let him take the easy road. She didn't make a sound. Ned wasn't sure where the decision came from; he wasn't trusting his own inspiration much at the moment. But he heard himself say, "Would you go out with me this weekend?"

"Dinner and a movie?"

"No. Just dinner. It's too hard to find a movie that I like anymore. And I'd rather have time to get better acquainted."

"Ned, those are magic words to me. I could kiss you right now—on our first phone call."

"Okay, but don't kiss me on our first date, all right?"

"I'll try to resist." Then after a couple of seconds she added,

"Actually, those are magic words too. I've had enough of those just-let-me-get-my-hands-on-you dates to last me for a lifetime."

"So what's best? Friday?"

"Friday is good. I'll leave Salt Lake a little earlier than usual. Let's start really early so we can talk for a long time. I've got a million things I want to know about you."

"Okay. So . . . what? Six?"

"Yeah. Old people eat dinner early. And then we can go for a drive or something."

"Six then. I'm looking forward to it. I had my heart set on family home evening, but dinner is good."

"Hey, I'm up for family home evening. We can do that too."

Ned didn't know whether she was kidding or not. Maybe he had two dates, not one, and he worried that if he didn't like her on Friday, the situation could be awkward. But he liked her right now, and he was even looking forward to answering all those questions she had for him—and asking a lot of his own. Strange, how exciting the thought of it was.

*Ned, you did a good thing. I like her.*

*Kate, don't show up now. It's embarrassing. If I think you're watching Friday night, I won't be able to say a thing.*

*Don't worry about it. I'm putting you on your own. But what was that crack about her being more straightforward than I am?*

*Oh, brother. I knew you wouldn't like that.*

*No, no. I'm fine. Good-bye, Ned. You're going to be okay now, and I really do need to leave you alone.*

But the "good-bye" scared Ned. He doubted he was ready for *that.*

# Chapter Eleven

✦

Ned spent seven hours with Carol on Friday evening, stayed up later than he had in a long time, and was amazed how quickly the time passed. On Sunday, at church, they didn't sit together or even say much to one another—since Ned didn't want to start any rumors—but on Monday night he drove over to her condo and they drank hot chocolate by her fire and talked about everything: their kids, their grandkids, their "interests," and even things Ned didn't tell most people. He talked about his frustration with retirement—the feelings he had experienced lately with his life having no meaning. Carol understood, but she expressed her own concern that life was a little too intense. She had bought the condo in Midway so she could feel the peace and beauty of the valley, and she had promised herself she would cut back on her hours in the store, but so far she hadn't been able to do that. The daily commute was already getting tiresome.

Ned kept realizing that the two of them were quite different in many ways. She leaned toward Democrats, she admitted, and some of her political positions were more liberal than his, but he liked the things she was concerned about even if she had reached different conclusions about how to deal with them. Or honestly, he couldn't get himself to care. He never had been very sure about answers to big questions. What he was feeling was that her heart was right, and her head was set on straight. Besides, it was a very nice head to look at, with pretty brown eyes. He also noticed that the neck and other structures that held that head up were not bad either.

But Ned came home frightened. He was feeling too familiar too fast. That had seemed okay when he was with her, but after, as he drove home, he didn't know quite what to think of what was happening. All this could lead to someone in his bathroom someday, drying her hair while he was stepping out of the shower. He just couldn't imagine anything that "familiar" in his life. Not again. No matter what he told himself, it seemed to be cheating on Kate even to think about it. And it was one thing to figure out intimacy as a young man, but the thought of doing that again—with a second woman—was embarrassing.

He remembered his wedding night with Kate when, after all their restraint, they knew it was okay to go to bed together. He had tried to be casual when they had checked into the hotel, like he wasn't actually nervous and eager and, in truth, scared. Just when the situation was getting hopelessly tense, and he was desperately trying to think what he was supposed to do or say, Kate had started to laugh. "Do you know what to do?" she had asked.

"I think I have a pretty good idea," Ned had told her, but then he had broken up too.

They were still giggling when they got into bed, and they never really stopped. It hadn't been very romantic, he supposed, but it was great fun. What he couldn't imagine was a second wedding night. If Kate said a single word to him, he would never be able to manage it.

There were also a lot of practical concerns that came to mind whenever he let himself think about an actual future with Carol. They would have nine kids between the two of them, and thirteen grandchildren. Would the kids like each other? Ned didn't even know how his sons felt about a remarriage. There would be a thousand decisions to make: where to live, whether Carol would continue her business, whether Ned would start another career, and . . . everything else. Ned realized that the one good thing about his life now was that it was simple, and a new marriage would be very complicated.

Every time Ned allowed himself to consider realities, a defense mechanism would kick in and he would say the same word: *slow. Take it slow.* But Carol had already told him that she didn't want to date for five years and then find out he was merely looking for a friend. In all their conversations, one thing seemed clear: She was thinking that he just might be right for her. That was frightening, so *slow* was the word that gave him comfort, but he was surprised that he wanted to see her every evening. He resisted, didn't make a big rush toward her, but when he wasn't with her he wished that he were. That was scary stuff.

On Friday night they went out again. They had a wonderful dinner at the Blue Boar Inn and then drove to Park City, where they strolled along Main Street and looked around in some of the shops. On the way back to Midway, Carol asked Ned if he wanted to go to Salt Lake with her the next day. He could take a look at the shop she ran, and then she would take him to lunch at a place she loved downtown. "Actually, I can't," he said. "Liz and David are coming up tomorrow. I don't know how I got so lucky."

"You've never really said why you don't like him, Ned. What's up with that?"

"Not like him? How could I not like him? He's the *cutest* boy I've ever seen."

"You said something like that once before. Is he prissy or something?"

"No, no. He was captain of his football team, star of his basketball team, hero of every team. He hits a golf ball across time zones."

"Ahhhh. Jealousy has raised its ugly head."

Ned was driving past Jordanelle Reservoir. There was enough moonlight to reveal its dark waters in the valley below. He looked in that direction and tried to sound casual as he said, "Not at all. He's twenty-three, going on fifteen. He's the child of light. If he ever bumps into reality, he'll wonder what it is."

"So he's too . . . what?"

"Religious."

She cocked her head curiously. "Are you serious? That seems a strange complaint coming from a former bishop. Are you saying that he's self-righteous?"

It was exactly the word Ned had used to explain his distaste for David, and yet, committing himself to it out loud would have made him uncomfortable. So he answered seriously. "Not really. But he goes at righteousness like he's in a competition and he won't be satisfied unless he wins. I wish he'd just relax. He hardly knows how to laugh."

"Okay. I know the type."

But that wasn't quite the whole story either. David could laugh, could even be quite witty. Ned didn't dare admit that, though. Instead, he said, "We could do family home evening together again, if you're interested."

"You know how to excite a woman. My place or yours, big fella?"

"Mine. I'll cook something, just to prove I can."

"If you're trying to convince me that you're perfect, you can lay off now. I'm already impressed."

It was an odd thing to say, given his thoughts of the last couple weeks about David, but Ned let it go.

On Saturday morning Ned got up wishing more than anything that he could drive to Salt Lake with Carol and not have to be there when David arrived. Still, arrive he did, early in the afternoon after Ned spent the morning cleaning again. And shortly after making their appearance, Liz found it convenient to slip away. Ned was caught in the great room with David, nowhere to run, nowhere to hide, and an obvious question— *the* obvious question—about to drip from his lips. Ned tried to engage him in a conversation about BYU football, but David fended off the delay, got an earnest look on his face, and began: "Brother Stevens."

Ned didn't bother to remind him to say, "Ned." It was hopeless.

"As you know, I'm in love with your daughter." He was standing in front of the fire in such a way that it glowed around him like an aura. David was coming forth in flame and light, and he would not be denied.

Ned more or less collapsed on the big couch straight across from David. And just so he wouldn't have to hear David's prepared speech, he said, "Yes, it's fine. You have my blessing. Go ahead and marry her."

David seemed not to hear what Ned had said. He had a speech prepared, and by darn, he was going to give it. "I haven't dated a lot of girls. I don't know why. It's just not something that appealed to me much. But I've always had lots of friends who were girls."

"Well, that's good. You probably know what you—"

"I think, though, when you meet the right girl, and you're in tune with the Spirit, you know. And there's not the slightest doubt in my mind that Liz is the right one for me. I want to give her a ring for Christmas, Brother Stevens, but I wouldn't feel right about asking her to marry me if you didn't feel good about it too. I know you have some doubts about me, and I don't blame you. I have plenty of doubts about myself. So maybe you need some time to think, but I do want to ask for her hand in marriage."

"David, I don't have doubts about you. I'm not going to hide the fact that I had some concerns at first, mainly because Liz is awfully young—at least in my mind—but you're a good young man and she's nuts about you. You're a 'great catch,' besides. I'm sure any father would be happy to have his daughter marry such a fine young man."

He had done the best he could, but he sensed that his voice didn't exactly ring with sincerity. There was still a stiffness between them, and Ned knew that David felt it too. Ned stood, stepped toward David, and gave him a good, sound handshake, and that was that. But David was actually looking more nervous than when he had started into the little scene, and they both knew why. Ned wasn't going to smack him on the back and tell him that this was the happiest day of his life.

David went to get Liz after that, and she came back trying to smile, but apparently imbued with some of David's discomfort. What had he said? Maybe, "Your dad said yes, but I can tell that he still doesn't like me." Something of that sort, Ned supposed. So he tried to do better with Liz. He hugged her tight and told her it was hard to accept that his little girl had grown up, and a few other platitudes—anything that sounded like something dads said at such a moment. But Liz wasn't squealing with delight, or crying, or bubbling over. She was as stiff as David. If Ned had ever needed Kate back, it was now, and some longing for that returned to him. He had allowed himself to get rather excited about Carol this last week, but what he really wanted was his wife, not someone new. He needed someone to kick him in the pants, if nothing else, because he was really botching this moment.

Everyone sat down, David and Liz close together on the other couch, and Ned asked the obvious question: "So what are your plans? When are you thinking that you want to get married?"

"We're not exactly sure," Liz said. "This summer, of course, before David has to leave for medical school, but we have to think about when. To tell you the truth, Dad, I told David that if you seemed really against this, I might have to wait for a while."

Sometimes Ned knew precisely what not to do and did it anyway. He never had understood that about himself. But he heard the words coming out of his mouth even though he knew the effect they would have. "You know, when you talk about waiting, I'm not so sure it would be a bad idea. If David got a year of medical school behind him, and you got a little closer to graduating, that might be a better plan. The first year of med school is supposed to be awful, and Liz, without a degree, you're not going to be able to help him much financially. You're both young enough that another year of experience and maturity couldn't hurt at all." By then Ned could see the devastated looks on their faces, and so he added, "I'm not saying that's what you should do. I'm just saying it's something to consider."

"Brother Stevens, I don't think I could stand that. I could never go away and leave Liz behind—not now."

"Daddy, when I thought we were going to have to stop dating—you know, that weekend that you got so upset—all I did was cry. I'm committed to David now, in my heart, and I don't ever want to be away from him again."

Ned had a sarcastic remark in his head: *How can I argue with logic like that?* But he didn't say it. He didn't even feel it. The fact was, he remembered how he had felt about Kate after he had asked her to marry him. To wait a year would have been like asking him to cut off a limb. These kids really did love each other, and only a pitiful old man would come up with the suggestion that they wait. Had he done it to be cruel or just because he saw a straw he could try to grab? In any case, he was embarrassed. "I know what you mean. I guess it is time for you two to be together."

"But Dad, you still don't seem happy about it."

"I am. It's just hard to see you head off to the East Coast or somewhere like that. Everyone will be gone now. But you're right, I do tend to cling to you."

*Ned, that was cheap. You know what you're up to.*

*So where were you when I needed you? Why show up now?*

*Just say something nice. Make them feel okay about this.*

"But you know what?" Ned said. "I stole your mom away and took her off to California. Grandma always felt bad about that. It's just the way life is. It's time for you two to make your own life together."

He thought he had said it pretty well, but Liz hadn't relaxed yet. "Dad, this is hurting me. You're just saying what you think you have to say. I know you still don't feel good about us getting married, and I don't know why. And don't tell me that it's because I'm too young. I don't believe that's your real concern." Tears had come into Liz's eyes now, and David slid his arm around her protectively.

Ned felt like the jerk he was, but she had asked for a real answer, so he allowed himself to consider. Why was he still resisting? He wasn't sure that the answer that came to him was *the* answer, but it was certainly one of them. "Liz, I haven't been able to get over the idea that you two are actually quite different. I still don't know whether you're right for each other."

"If we don't feel that way, why should you?"

So Ned dug into his brain again, even searched around in his chest. "We're not so . . . uptight . . . in our family. I want to spoil my grandchildren. You know, give them a good old-fashioned, materialistic, wrong-spirited Christmas. I can't go up against the Markham family logic. One gift ought to be plenty, but I want to give more than that. I want them to have a bunch of stuff on Christmas morning, and then know very well that they'll pick up some more from me. I want them to talk to their cousins about the big haul they got. It's the American way. It's probably wrong, but I love it."

What surprised Ned most was that David was smiling. Ned looked at him quizzically. "I'm sorry," David said, "but Liz and I already had this conversation. We agreed we would figure something out that wasn't quite so extreme either way." But then he looked more serious. "The thing you have to understand is that my family is painfully materialistic. We have the house and cars and the clothes to prove it—as you pointed out. But we're trying to fight some of that. After Dad received his calling, he dropped his membership in the country club because it seemed too showy, and he started to look around for some things he could do with his money. We all talked about it, that we were living this life of self-indulgence. We felt guilty about it. If you want to worry about me, worry that my real values will show through, and our kids will be spoiled."

"But that day we were shopping, you sounded so cheap. I wanted to buy my daughter some nice things, and you made me feel guilty about it."

"Okay, Dad," Liz said, "I'm going to tell you something—even though David doesn't want me to." She glanced at David, and he looked confused, or maybe concerned. "When I first got to know David, I couldn't believe what a penny-pincher he was. People had told me that he came from a wealthy family, but he wouldn't spend a dime."

"Liz, don't get into all that," David said, sounding rather stern.

But Liz plowed ahead, ignoring him. "Then I found out that he's paying the expenses not just for himself but for his roommate—an old missionary companion. This guy was out of money and was going to drop out of school, so David said he'd cover him this year—you know, his rent and food. He does all that with the money his dad sends him for his own expenses."

"It's just a loan," David said. "He's going to pay me back."

"But see, this is just the thing," Ned said. He rested his ankle across his knee and leaned back. He didn't want bad feel-ings, but he had to say this. "David, once again, I'm convinced you're a saint. You live on some other plane from the rest of us. But I've raised Liz as an average American girl—self-indulgent, self-centered, a little vain. You know, normal. If you two get married, you're going to drive each other crazy. I'd like just once to hear that you have a weakness, that you have some sort of human tendencies. Every time I think I find a fault, it's explained away by some act of self-sacrifice. Can't you give me an example of a time you gave in to temptation—maybe ate a whole ice cream cone or secretly longed to punch some guy in the nose?"

"You don't know me, Brother Stevens."

"Do you have to call me 'brother' all the time?"

"You don't know me, Ned. I'm not—"

"Do you ever eat a big old hamburger, with fries?"

"Well . . . not really. I have done . . . but not for a while."

Ned let out a gust of breath.

But Liz jumped in. "You don't eat junk food either, Dad. So quit pointing fingers."

"But it's a fight for me. And I slip once in a while."

"So that's David's problem, that he holds to the things he believes?"

"That's exactly his problem."

"But Brother Stevens—really—you've got the wrong idea about me."

"I do? Okay, Brother Markham, unload on me. Tell me something really bad you've done—just once."

David let go of Liz. He leaned forward, rested his elbow on his knees, and hung his head. Ned was suddenly frightened. Maybe the kid had done something horrible, and he was about to spill it.

"I know that I annoy people, Ned. I've known it for a long time. But I'm not sure how to change myself. When I was growing up, my father was always telling me, 'Where much is given, much is expected.' He would tell me how many gifts I had, and if I didn't use them, it would show my ungratefulness to the Lord. But the truth is, I'm kind of lazy, and I lose interest in things. I can usually learn something pretty fast, and there are quite a few things I can do pretty well, but I work at a skill for a while and then something else catches my attention. I always felt, growing up, like I was letting everyone down. I did okay at most things, but someone always seemed to expect more. My coaches would chew me out for not going all out at practice, or my seminary teacher would tell me that I had to be a better example to the other Mormon kids. For a long time, I didn't buy into all that. I was pretty cocky about the stuff I had done with ninety percent effort. I don't think I even knew that I wasn't trying my full-on best."

"So you're telling me you were arrogant. That was your weakness?"

"No. I'm telling you I'm still arrogant. That will always be my weakness, and that's why I fight it so hard. My mission president called me into his office and told me that I was supposed to be a mission leader but that the other missionaries didn't like me. I was acting like a hotshot, bragging all the time. So I made up my mind to do better. It's something I'm working on all the time. Lately, I've been trying to do some things for other people, just so I won't center all my thoughts on myself."

"So you work at the homeless shelter and sing at rest homes just to prove to yourself that you're not such a bad guy."

"Maybe. I guess that's probably right, even if I don't want to think of it that way. I read in the scriptures that Christ says to forget yourself and serve people. But then people find out I've done something like that, and they think I'm trying to make myself look good. I end up annoying people no matter what I do."

Liz put her arm around David's shoulders and looked at Ned. "Dad, has it occurred to you yet that this is a ridiculous conversation? You're trying to get David to convince you that he's got enough faults that he qualifies to marry me. David's dad ought to be calling me on his carpet and asking that I step my life up a notch just to be worthy of someone like David."

That very thought had occurred to Ned. But he didn't buy it—not entirely.

"Let me tell you what I've learned about David, Dad. He hungers and thirsts after righteousness. And people make him feel bad for doing that."

Ned was struck with that thought. It did seem to explain David, and Ned felt a little shame. So he tried to explain himself. "You are a good young man, David. I guess I just want to know that you're made out of the same stuff as the rest of us—that you have to struggle with personal challenges the way everyone else does. You tell me you have to deal with arrogance, but it seems to me you've triumphed, and done it rather easily. You made up your mind and you did it. Normal people can't seem to do that."

David looked up, seemingly surprised, but Liz was laughing. "Oh, Dad, just give him time. He'll show you how vain he still is."

Ned looked at David, who was shaking his head and smiling. "You don't have to tell him about that."

"Yes, I do. He and his partner won this debate championship, so he—"

"You're on the debate team, too?"

"Yeah. Didn't we tell you that?"

"No." Ned couldn't keep his eyes from rolling, but Liz didn't seem to notice.

"Anyway, they took his picture for the student paper, and he didn't like the picture; he had one at home he liked better, so he hurried down to the *Daily Universe* office to try to replace the one he didn't like. When they told him he was too late, he asked to see the faculty advisor, and he got in a big argument with the girl at the desk when she wouldn't let him."

"But you'd have to see this picture, Brother Stevens. It was really goofy looking."

Ned was laughing. He liked this story. "You got in an argument with the girl?"

"It was worse than that," Liz said. "This guy on the staff came up and started defending the girl, and David asked the guy if he wanted to go outside and have it out."

Ned was joyous. "No kidding. You did that?"

"Yes, but I've worked really hard on my temper since then. I got in a lot of fights in high school. Guys were always calling me out, and I wasn't going to back down. But when you read the Sermon on the Mount, you can see how wrong that attitude is. I'm trying—"

"But you were going to duke it out with this guy?"

David grinned. "It wouldn't have been much of a fight. This little newsboy had a big mouth, but he weighed about 150. One punch, and he would have been down."

Ned was staring now.

"But I'm glad he wouldn't go outside with me. I mean, violence like that is really stupid."

"True, true." But Ned was smiling at David now, and David couldn't seem to stop grinning himself.

"I'll tell you something else," Liz said. "David always seems really organized and on top of things. But it's all show. He forgets things. He stood me up twice this fall, and both times just because he was doing something else and lost track of time. He puts everything in his Palm Pilot, and then he forgets to look at it."

"You told me he's always on time."

"He is, if he remembers. But he spaces things out. And he's accident prone. He's wrecked his car twice since school started."

"How can you tell?" Ned asked.

David grinned again. "That's one of the reasons I drive that car. But I didn't get in a big smashup or anything. I just back up sometimes and don't notice what's behind me."

"Your mind's on bigger issues," Ned said.

"That's what I tell my dad, but he says that I need to come down from the stars and focus on reality."

"So does he think you're a little too . . . what? . . . philosophical?"

"No. He thinks I'm a flake. He's worried I'll get halfway through med school and lose interest. He says I don't ever finish things."

Ned reacted rather more than he wanted to. "Is it possible that would be a problem?"

"No. It won't be. I've made up my mind about that."

"And I've warned him," Liz said. "If he quits med school, I quit him."

But this actually sounded serious. It had never occurred to Ned that he might have to worry about this boy. The fact was, he rather liked the change. In fact, he found himself thinking that he could get to like David if he would keep laughing and maybe do something stupid once in a while.

"But Daddy, David's heart is so good. I know it seems like he's uptight. But he studies the scriptures and he takes them seriously. Isn't that what we're supposed to do?"

"Yes. It is. We all should hunger and thirst after righteousness." Ned nodded at David, but David was looking down again.

*You need to think this one over, Ned. The poor guy is embarrassed by his righteousness, and you're the guy who's been keeping the pressure on him.*

*I know. I am* thinking *about it.*

But right now Ned was feeling a lot better about David—and he was especially tired of all this awkwardness. It was time to change the subject. So he asked, "Do you two think you could help me with something while you're here?"

"What's that?" Liz asked.

"My Christmas tree. I bought a big, tall one—you know, artificial—but it has lights on it, and the directions look really complicated—lots of plugs and things. I've got a tall enough ladder, but I'm not sure I can assemble the thing by myself."

"Sure. We can help," David said.

"But wait a minute," Liz said, "are we engaged, or what?"

"Well, yuhhhh," Ned said. "You need to stay up with the conversation, honey."

"I'll ask you officially later, okay?" David said to Liz. "I'll make it really nice."

"But shouldn't we . . . I don't know . . . kiss or something?"

"I don't think that's necessary," Ned said. "I don't believe in kissing out of wedlock." But then he walked out to the deck to get the two big boxes the tree had come in. Since David didn't follow, that seemed to indicate that the boy was willing to fulfill his duty, as usual.

❁   ❁   ❁

The Christmas tree turned into more of a project than Ned had imagined. It was easy enough to see the order of the four sections of the tree; it was following the diagram and plugging

in all the electrical cords that proved a nightmare. After everything seemed to be installed correctly, red plug in red receptacle,
blue in blue, and so on, Ned plugged the master cord into the
wall socket, and there was light. Mostly. One big section, three-
fourths of the way to the top, remained dark. It was exactly what
Ned had expected. He could never make anything like this
work. David began to check out the trail of cords, comparing
the diagram in the instructions. Ned was glad to let him take
over—and it was nice to think the boy might be around every
year for Christmas so he could save Ned's bacon.

David had climbed toward the top of the ten-foot "Little
Giant" ladder when he finally announced, "Okay, I think this is
our problem right here. I think this cord is plugged into the
wrong line." He reached into the center of the tree but couldn't
seem to get hold of the plug. He slipped more to the edge of
the ladder, shifted his weight, and then reached again.

"Can we move the ladder a little?" Ned was asking.

"No, it's okay. I've almost got it."

And then he leaned just a little more.

The disaster didn't come suddenly; it was all sort of slow
motion. As the ladder began to tip, David tried to swing his
weight back, but it was too late, and he rode the thing into the
tree, which held for a moment but soon began to tip as well
under David's weight. David was flailing, trying to grab something, and then, finally, seemed to make an effort to jump. But
his footing was gone by then, and there was a grand, long crash,
as tree, David, and ladder slowly toppled over. Ned could hear
the limbs smash, but his eyes were on David, who rolled with
the tree and then broke free and crashed to the floor. The ladder
landed on top of the tree, not on David, but David hit with a

great thud, on his side, before rolling onto his back. For a moment, he didn't move.

Liz got to him first, but Ned was close behind. "Are you all right?" they were both shouting into his face.

David stared back at them, as though he were waiting for the answer himself, maybe waiting for pain to show up somewhere. But after a few seconds, he said, "Yeah, I'm okay. But I'm not so sure about the tree."

Another three or four seconds passed, and Ned tried to worry about his tree, but he couldn't stop himself. He started to laugh. And then Liz did too. And finally David.

"Hey, Dave," Ned said, "I thought you were some kind of genius fix-it man."

"I told you, Liz exaggerates."

"Boy, are you telling me? From now on, I'll put my own tree together—if you haven't ruined it. You're a real flake, you know it?"

Everyone stayed on the floor and laughed for a good while, and it crossed Ned's mind that he hadn't laughed this well, or felt this happy, in a very long time.

# Chapter Twelve

❋

David and Liz stayed overnight and then went to church with Ned in the morning. Ned was careful to avoid Carol. Liz didn't know about any of that, and he didn't want her to know. If nothing came of this whole thing, it would be just as well that his family never knew that it had ever happened. And if he did tell Liz, she would be all over him, pushing and shoving him down the aisle before he even knew the woman.

The truth was, Ned had agreed to have Sunday dinner with Carol at her condo. He had promised to call her as soon as the kids headed home, and she said she wouldn't start cooking until he called. He feared he might have to fix a meal for David and Liz and then drop over to Carol's for a later dinner. But David had to get back, they said, so after church they stayed only long enough to gather their things.

Liz gave Ned a big hug and thanked him for everything, and Ned felt good about that. Then there was David, with his arms stretched out, and Ned did his duty. He gave David lots of hard backslaps, which was always the way to prove that it was a real man's hug and not anything too touchy-feely. But David told him, "I think we had a little breakthrough last night, Brother Stevens. It's something we can build on."

True, true. But he didn't have to say it. Sometimes it was

better not to use a lot of words and just move ahead. Clearly, Ned felt better about David, but the guy would be showing up for the rest of Ned's life just long enough to beat his brains out on the golf links. At least Ned had something to worry about: The lazy bum might drop out of med school. Ned just hoped the boy would "get it all together" someday and not be quite such a slouch. These were such comforting thoughts. All through church, Ned had been remembering that lovely word *flake*. Ned could never truly dislike David again after hearing him called that. And who should know better than the boy's own father?

David had no more sense than to wrap his arms around Ned, call him brother, and say kindly things in his ear—but he meant well. That's what Ned always wanted to remember. David was just trying very hard to get life right. If the Lord could forgive him for his sins, surely Ned could forgive him for his perfections. One could balance out the other, and Ned and David could get through life together without too much pain. Still, Ned was going to buy a new golf club he had read about in *Golf Magazine*—guaranteed to add twenty yards to his drive. If Ned bought that driver, maybe got the weight-lifting equipment he was thinking about, and worked really hard on his short game, there was a chance that David could become downright charming in time.

So the kids left, and Ned called Carol. "The coast is clear," he said. "They took off already."

"I'll bet you didn't tell them you were coming over here, though, did you?"

"No."

"And you avoided me at church."

"Yes."

"What am I, your secret woman? Your dalliance?"

"No. But you know how Liz is. If I say anything—"

"Yeah, yeah, yeah. You're ashamed of me. But when are you coming over?"

"You say."

"Right now. You can talk to me while I cook."

"Should I bring a salad, or—"

"No. I've got salad stuff. Good stuff. Come over and you can help me make it up."

"Okay, I'll just change clothes, and then I'll head over."

"Ned?"

"Yes."

"Are you thinking about kissing me today?"

"No. It's the Sabbath."

"It's not fast Sunday." Ned liked that one. He laughed, and she did too. But he wasn't going to kiss her. For one thing, he couldn't remember any moves. He wasn't sure how a guy went from talking—even sitting next to a woman on the couch—to bending around and going for it. But that wasn't his greatest concern. He was afraid she was going to make the move, as she teased him at times she was likely to do, and he wasn't ready for that. Kate had told him she wanted him to marry, but he didn't think she would like the idea that he was going out with one woman after another, kissing them all. He wasn't going to kiss anyone until he knew exactly what his intentions were, and his goal, for the present, was to avoid intentions.

Ned drove up to Carol's condo on the hillside. His only concern was that a lot of people who lived up there were in his ward. He was afraid they would spot him sneaking in, or know his car. So he drove his Honda, which people didn't know as well as the Land Rover. After he parked, he hurried inside, ran up the stairs without seeing anyone, and was relieved to get inside the door without being discovered.

But Carol knew exactly what he had done. "Did you wear a ski mask or anything, just long enough to get upstairs?"

"No, I wore glasses. The kind with eyebrows and a nose."

"Oh, I see that you did. Go ahead and take them off now."

"You are such a wit."

She smiled, flooding the room. He tried to remember why that smile had annoyed him so much at one time.

"Wow. What smells so good?"

"It's my new cologne. It's called Pot Roast." She walked over and peeked into the oven through the glass, then opened the door a little and took a better look. "I hope this thing turns out all right. It's my attempt to show you that I'm domestic, but I haven't cooked one of these in years."

"It's strange how people cook when they're alone, isn't it?"

They both seemed to know what the statement meant, but maybe it sounded a little like a suggestion that cooking for two would be better. Whatever it meant to her, she took a long look at him, and Ned suddenly realized how homey this was: Carol wearing an apron over the pretty green dress she had worn to church, and the two of them in the kitchen. After Ned's boys had left home, and Liz was off running around, there had been so many times, on Sunday, or on a weekday evening, that Ned and Kate had been alone. They had put together a sandwich and some soup, or something just as simple, sat at the table and talked, and then, most of the time, sat together in the family room and read or watched the news together on TV. It had never seemed terribly significant, just pleasant most of the time, but it was what life was to Ned. He remembered it now that he was seeing it again.

Ned hadn't bothered to change his clothes, really. He had taken off his tie and slipped on a gray V-neck sweater over his white shirt. But he had worn a leather jacket, not his suit coat, and now the inside pocket in that jacket had begun to ring. He thought it was Carol's phone for a moment, but then recognized his Beethoven's Fifth ring and fished his cell phone out.

"Hello," he said, unable to imagine who would call him on his cell on a Sunday afternoon.

"Dad. Oh good. I'm glad I found you." It was Liz. "Where did you go? I tried to call the house and you weren't there."

Ned decided not to answer that one. "What's the trouble?"

"We're in a bit of a mess. We need your help."

"Where are you?"

"We're almost to the mouth of Provo Canyon." She hesitated, but then she said, "I know you don't want to hear this, but we came on a car that had crashed into the Provo River. David jumped in the river and pulled everyone out—a woman and seven kids—but he's really wet and cold now."

"Are you kidding me?"

"Yes."

"Oh."

"But you believed me, didn't you?"

"Well . . . yeah. A little."

"It's nothing like that. We ran over something in the road and we've got a flat tire. David got in his trunk to get his spare, and there isn't one. He doesn't know what happened to it, or whether he ever had one. I could kill the guy sometimes."

"Hey, it's all right. People make mistakes. Especially that guy." Ned was grinning now, his chest swelling with joy.

"Could you drive down and help us? I tried to call some friends in Provo, but I couldn't find anyone home."

"Hey, sure. I'll be right down. I'll bring my Honda. The spare out of it ought to be the same size. If it works, you can just take that for now. But it's going to take me half an hour to get there. Are you two warm?"

"I'm warm, and if I let David stay in the car, he'll be okay. But I'm thinking about kicking him out. He's such a lame brain."

"Now, now. Be merciful. You might do something incredibly stupid yourself someday."

Liz was giggling, and so was Ned. And Carol was looking at Ned as though she wondered what in the world he was talking about. He punched off the phone and said, "I've got to go help David and Liz. That David is a complete flake. I don't know how Liz puts up with him."

Carol smiled, probably in response to Ned's continuing grin, but she said, "What's this all about? Isn't this the guy you were calling 'angel boy' the other day? And 'matchless light'?"

"Yeah. But I had him all wrong. He gets into one mess after another. I have to save his muffins all the time."

Carol was clearly not getting this, but Ned had to go.

"Look, it'll be at least an hour before I get back. Is there a way to slow down that roast?"

"I can just turn the heat down. It might get dry, but at least I'll have an excuse if it isn't any good."

"Okay. Turn it down, and I'll make it back as fast as I can."

"I want to go with you."

"Oh. Uh . . . you better watch that roast."

"What's it going to do?"

"Get dry, or—"

"It can do that without me. I'd rather ride down with you than sit here alone."

"I know. But you know Liz. She'll make a big deal out of this."

Carol had stepped to the oven and twisted the knob, and now she was taking her apron off. "Ned, if you apologize right now, I'll still ride down the canyon with you. Otherwise, a woman could start to take your attitude as an insult."

Ned used up the better part of ten seconds trying to think of something to say, but he had known immediately that he had lost this one. "Okay. I'm sorry. Ride down with me. But let's just tell Liz that we're friends."

Carol smiled, floridly. "Okay. We won't tell her the truth."

"I didn't mean that. We *are* just friends. But—"

"But you like me and I like you. It's our little secret."

Ned had no idea what to do with this woman sometimes, but she had him smiling again, and she did look pretty. "Do you think you ought to turn the roast off? If we got delayed some way—"

"Ahh, let's just take a chance. Let's live on the wild side."

But downstairs—after they had looked both ways and made a run for the car—Carol told him, "I've got to stop being quite so much of a smart aleck. I think I get under your skin sometimes."

"All I ask is that you stop telling the truth. I learned to date the old-fashioned way, where I had to watch for little signals. All this straight talk throws me out of my game."

"Do you really feel that way? I mean, do I embarrass you?"

"Do you embarrass me? Yes. Do I want to play it the other way? No. I think you're what's called 'refreshingly honest.'"

"Not all the time. You just bring the worst out in me."

"Why?"

"I don't know. It's funny to watch you get flustered—and

you look so cute when you blush. But tell me when enough is enough. I really don't want to scare you off. I do think we need time to get to know each other better, no matter how much I tease you. If you weren't so hesitant, I probably would be."

"So what's your favorite color?"

"What?"

"I'm getting to know you better." They had reached downtown Midway—all of it in one block, more or less. The chime on the town hall was playing, even though it wasn't really 2:30 as the clock said it was. So much for fine Swiss instruments.

"I can never decide about colors," Carol said. "I think I like all of them. How do people pick one?"

"You *are* complex."

"Well, which one do you like best?"

"Blue," Ned told her.

"Why blue?"

"Because I started saying it in third grade, or somewhere along about then, and then I just stuck with it."

"You *are* simple."

He glanced at her, smiled, and then asked what he really wanted to know: "What kind of an accounting system do you use in that store of yours?"

He got the answer he sort of hoped for: She had no idea. It was what Kate would have said.

They drove past Deer Creek Reservoir and on down the canyon, finally spotting David's car pulled over to the side. It looked like an abandoned pile of scrap metal. The tire had gone flat in a four-lane section of the highway, where pulling off hadn't been the problem that it might have been higher up the canyon. Ned pulled up behind the old car and began to say, "If you just want to sit in the—" but Carol was already out of the car by then.

So Ned hurried, trying to get to David's car before Carol did, but David and Liz were by then getting out on both sides. And suddenly there they were, four of them, the two women facing each other, and the two men. Both David and Liz were staring straight at Carol.

"I've got that spare in the back," Ned almost shouted, trying to pull Liz's eyes to him, but Liz was looking mystified, or maybe in awe, as though she were seeing some natural wonder for the first time. "Carol," she finally said.

"Hi, Liz. Is this David?" Carol cut between the cars and shook David's hand. Ned could see that she was trying to make this seem natural. "My name's Carol Holly. I'm in Ned's ward. We're friends." But then she beamed, and David beamed back at her, both setting off special effects with their teeth.

"Let's get that spare," Ned was saying, "and see if it—"

But Liz was on her way around the car now, homing in on Carol like a guided missile. A big truck rushed by, drowning the sound out, but as soon as it roared away, Liz said, "So that's where Dad was. Have you two been hanging out together or something?"

Carol laughed; then she seemed to make a valiant effort on Ned's behalf. "A little," she said, but she couldn't contain the sparkle.

"Are you *going out?*"

Carol glanced at Ned, and he tried to tell her with his eyes to deny all such accusations, but Ned could see that Carol was losing a battle with herself.

"I wouldn't say going out . . ." Ned began.

207

But at the same moment, Carol was spilling the beans. "Yes, we are."

"Holy cow! Really?"

"Yes, and I think he likes me."

"Has he kissed you?"

*Please don't do this.*

"No. But I keep telling him I'm ready whenever he is."

*Oh, brother. Now I'm in for it.*

"I'll tell you what to do," Liz shouted as a pair of cars buzzed by. "When he walks you to your door, step right up close to him, turn your head a little so he has a clear shot, shut your eyes, and stretch your neck toward him."

"Does that work?"

"It finally worked on David, but only after the third try, and that time I also took hold of him around the waist and pulled him toward me. He says that I kissed him, but I deny it. I only *hinted*."

"Well, it's worth a try. I'll let you know how it turns out."

"Carol, I am so happy. Don't give up on him. He's like the slowest learner in the world. But sooner or later he catches on to things."

"About that tire," Ned was saying to David. "Shall we see whether it will work?"

But David was grinning at him like he knew something. Everyone was. At the moment, Ned didn't like any of them.

The wheel did fit, and Ned escaped the situation as fast as he could, but the whole time David and Ned were changing the tire, Carol and Liz were sitting in the Honda, talking. It had never occurred to Ned before, but the two reminded him of each other. They looked nothing alike, but they seemed charged with the same spunky energy, and they were both terrible about teasing him. They also both possessed the same ability to point at the emperor in his underwear even when everyone else in the room was pretending not to notice. Ned knew where Liz had learned that trait, too.

Meanwhile, back at the condo, the roast did turn out a little dry, but all in all, quite tasty. Carol had done some nice things with seasoning, and she had thought of interesting ingredients for her salad. Ned especially liked the pine nuts. He also liked that their talk turned serious, and Ned told her some things he needed to say. He told her about Kate, what she had meant to him, and what he had gone through since she died. Carol seemed to like him for his love for her, and she talked about the sorrow she felt for the man she had loved so much as a college girl, and for the loss of him—not so much the divorce, but the gradual loss, as she felt him change and grow more distant. Ned admitted that he talked to Kate sometimes and kept her close to him that way. He also told Carol he wanted to move slowly in his relationship with her, not because of some deep-rooted reticence, but merely because he was having to get used to the idea of having feelings for anyone else.

"Does it make you feel guilty?" Carol asked.

"Yes."

"But she told you she wanted you to get married."

"I know."

"I understand. I think I would feel the same way. But let me tell you what's a whole lot worse. When your spouse leaves you for someone else, you look inside yourself and say, 'There must be something wrong with me. I still loved him, and he stopped loving me.'"

"Do you still love him?"

"I love the man I married. I don't love the one who doesn't

bother much with his own children and grandchildren, and then pops up from time to time expecting everyone to be happy to see him. I married a boy, Ned, and he stayed a boy. One of the things I like about you is that you grew up to be a man. And you know how to be a father. Liz practically worships you."

"I haven't done the greatest job lately. I've acted like a teenager."

"She understands. She knows what you've been going through."

When Ned left that night, rather late, considering that he had arrived in the middle of the day, he half expected Carol to step up to him, turn her head to the correct position, and shut her eyes. He wasn't really sure what he might have done, had she done so. But she didn't, and he was relieved.

When he got home, he stood on the deck in the dark, with stars so thick they were like a smear across the sky, and said, *Kate, I hope this is okay.*

She didn't say anything, but he felt something brush against him, maybe a breeze.

*I'll still follow, later. All right? This doesn't change things between us.*

# Chapter Thirteen

It was Christmas Eve. Over the last few days, Ned's three sons had arrived with their families. John and his wife, Lori, were home from Belgium with their three children. Nate and Gina and their little boy, Daniel, had driven down from Portland. And Jerry, who was in graduate school in Chapel Hill, North Carolina, had flown in just the day before with his wife, Carly, and their two little boys. The house was full of people, in every bedroom, and there were beds on the floor of the family room and in the loft. No one seemed to go to bed. The parents watched movies on the big screen and stayed up late, and babies were crying long before the sun was up in the morning. Ned would lie in bed and hear showers running or toilets flushing at seemingly every hour of the night. But he loved it all. Life seemed full, even overcrowded, but familiar and right.

The six grandkids ran through the house banging doors and scaring Ned, worrying him that they would break something, or break themselves. Madeleine, who was five, would get angry with her three-year-old brother Neddy and cousin Daren because they kept bothering her when she was trying to "watch her shows" on the TV in the loft. The three littler cousins—Gabe, Isadore, and Daniel—all between ages one and two, loved to be read to, or at least liked to sit on Grandpa's lap, but they sometimes resented each other for getting Ned's attention first. Ned could hold two of them or even all three—with a little ingenuity—and he loved every second of that. He knew that when everyone finally headed home, he would welcome the return of peace, but he also knew that the quiet would be hard to get used to again.

Lori and Carly had relatives in Utah, so those families would be gone at least part of the next day, on Christmas, but everyone would be together tonight. The three daughters-in-law had started a turkey that afternoon, the smell filling the house and mixing with the aroma of hot rolls and pies. Ned thought of Kate, who had always wanted two ovens and a warming drawer but had never had them. The girls had all three now, and they told Ned how wonderful it was. He had never used the warming drawer, but he was glad to know it worked, and he loved all the good smells the ovens could produce at the same time.

Ned had done a little decorating, with Liz's help, and had bent the Christmas tree limbs back into shape as best he could. He had even sorted out the wiring—with directions, not help, from David—and the lights all worked. Long ago, Kate had cross-stitched beautiful Christmas stockings for the kids, and later, had started to do them for the grandchildren. She had gotten only three done, but Ned had found some cute stockings for the little ones and had them all hanging from the fireplace mantel. Kate would have been proud, he thought, of how nice things looked.

Ned loved to watch his sons with their kids. They seemed closer to their children than he had been with them—more involved with diapers and bottles, and more knowledgeable about formula and ointments for diaper rash. This afternoon the men had been assigned to keep the kids out of the kitchen while their wives cooked, and they were doing pretty well. Ned kept trying to help in the kitchen, at least by finding mixing bowls and trays and special dishes, but he would, from time to time, slip downstairs to see how the guys were doing. They had a DVD going—*Monsters, Inc.*—and Jerry was holding little Gabe, both asleep in one of the recliners. Ned watched them for a while, thinking, "My little boy *has* a little boy, and he's a good dad." Jerry had never seemed the type to be domesticated, but here he was with two kids, acting as though it all came naturally. Kate would have loved to see this, dad and son, both breathing deeply, rolled up together. Maybe she *could* see it. Maybe she was seeing all of this, and maybe she was happy with the way things were going. Ned hoped so.

Not everything was perfect. Nate was still struggling with the Church. He had been a somewhat reluctant missionary, who had always had a lot of questions and doubts, and Gina, his wife—who had a lovely, simple faith—had talked to Ned the night before. She admitted that Nate skipped priesthood meeting half the time, just because he disagreed with so many things he heard there. So there was that to worry about, and Neddy, John's son, was still struggling with asthma. The climate in Belgium wasn't the best for him, and John had talked to Ned about giving up a very good job in order to get back to dry old Utah. He and Lori had been praying constantly about it, he told Ned, but John just wasn't sure he had an answer yet. He asked Ned how he could know for sure when the Lord was speaking to him. Ned always felt inadequate at such times. He had never found an easy formula. It always seemed that he made decisions, not quite sure of himself, and felt secure that he had received guidance only after things turned out okay. How did that help a young man trying to make a tough decision?

Just when it seemed the smells in the house couldn't get any better, the doorbell rang, and Ned opened the door to Carol. She brought in a subtle scent of White Linen—the cologne she wore and Ned liked so much—and with it, the equally enticing smell of a rhubarb pie. Ned loved rhubarb pie, and no one else did, so the daughters-in-law hadn't baked one, but someone must have tipped off Carol. Even though her pie was covered with a cloth, Ned knew the smell, and he took the treat and thanked her. They were just around the corner from the kitchen, still out of sight, so he leaned over and kissed her on the cheek, but she didn't let him get away with that. She gave him a nicer little kiss, on the lips. This was nothing new. A week or so back, he had taken her home one night, and Carol had teasingly taken him by the hand, pumped it several times, and said, "Thank you, Brother Stevens, for another wonderful evening."

It seemed the moral equivalent of a game of "chicken" or even an accusation that he was a wimp. But Ned knew when to rise up and proclaim himself a man. He had taken hold of her shoulders and pulled her slowly forward—as she continued to smile. Then her eyes had closed and her head had turned, and the kiss had seemed as natural as his love was becoming. He had given the kiss a little more "oomph" than he might have, maybe to impress her and put aside any suggestion of his lack of manliness. Or maybe it was just because he had loved the time they had spent together and he had been looking at those pretty lips all evening. In any case, she had stepped back afterward with her eyes rather wide, and she had said, "Wow. That was worth waiting for."

He had felt about a foot taller as he walked down the stairs, and almost hoped he would run into someone from the ward.

The rumors were running rampant by then anyway, and the bishop had called him just to say, "Way to go, Ned."

Ned took Carol's coat, and the two stepped around the little wall at the entrance. Ned loved what happened next. His sons' wives had known Carol only a few days, but she had slipped into the family so easily that everyone was comfortable with her already. They all hugged her, even though they had seen her the night before, and then, instantly, they were talking about dinner, about the pie, about Carol's pretty red dress. Carol walked to the china racks in the kitchen cabinets and started getting out the nice china.

All Ned's sons, all his daughters-in-law, had offered him the same advice, singly or two at a time: "Marry her, Dad. She's perfect for you." And John had told him, "She's nothing at all like Mom, and yet, so much the same I can hardly believe it."

"They have different personalities, but they're both open books," Ned told him. "I can't believe how well I know her already."

When Liz and David arrived, dinner was almost ready, and the big table—plus a card table—were set. David was staying in Utah for Christmas, and then, before New Year's, Liz was flying with him to Connecticut.

Liz came in looking like a spirit from a higher realm. She was smiling at least as brightly as David, and her face was flushed with more than cold. Ned knew what had happened, of course, but he would have been able to guess. She was wearing her black dress coat—the one that Ned was going to replace with cashmere in the morning—and black leather gloves. "Where are my brothers?" she asked.

"Downstairs," Ned told her.

She walked to the door and yelled down the stairs, "John

and Nate and Jerry, get up here immediately. There's an emergency. Abandon the kids and save yourselves."

They appeared before long, smiling—probably already aware of what was about to happen—and with most of the grandchildren trailing. The kids all loved Liz—and David. Liz's voice was usually enough to bring them all charging to her.

Liz struck a pose, like a model at the end of a runway, her left hand in the air. Once everyone was looking and smiling, she slowly pulled at each finger of her glove—a little too much like a striptease dancer, Ned thought—and then pulled off the glove to reveal the shining ring. It was materialistically large, in Ned's judgment—which made him laugh—but it looked rather dim compared to Liz's bright blue eyes, bright smile, bright everything. She was so beautiful, so happy, and Ned was happy for her. He got to her first, hugged her, and in a moment of unexpected excitement, hugged David too. Then he said, "Is that the only gift you're going to give her, you cheapskate?"

"No. We made a deal. This year we're spending Christmas with you, so we'll start our more moderate Christmases next year. I spent more money than I should have—and my parents sent her some stuff too. Don't tell anyone."

"It's our secret."

"Ned, you just can't believe how much my parents love Liz."

But Ned was looking at her again, watching her embrace everyone, with tears running down her cheeks. "No. I can believe it," he said.

The dinner was great, except that Isadore, a.k.a. "Issy," was getting tired and cranky, and started crying for no particular reason, and Neddy stole a black olive—the last one—off Daren's plate, and Daren tried to poke Neddy's eye out with his fork.

Fortunately, he missed, and Ned found another can of olives in the pantry. The two little boys, both three-year-olds, consumed almost all of them. They left turkey and mashed potatoes and salad and green beans on their plates, and had to hear warnings about starving children in various lands—all pronounced by Ned's facetious progeny in imitation of speeches they claimed Ned had given them in their youth—but the boys stuffed themselves with olives and sated any remaining hunger with lemon meringue pie. A little later—to no one's surprise—Neddy vomited all over the family room carpet, and Ned couldn't remember ever seeing anything so disgusting, but Neddy soon felt better, and everything was as it should be. Ned read the Christmas story in Luke, and the kids acted it out, and Issy, who had fallen asleep, made a perfect Christ child in her sister Madeleine's arms.

It was all rather disorganized and noisy, but it was peaceful in some way too, and Ned felt a wonderful fulness inside. He was thankful for Christ's birth in a way that he had never quite experienced before.

The men were assigned after the program to wash the dishes, and they didn't complain, probably because they preferred that to getting the kids ready for bed. But just as Ned was rolling up his sleeves, Liz came after him and dragged him outside onto the deck. There had finally been some snow, and everything was white outside. The night was quiet, with enough moon to create a glow on the trees and on the rolling contours of the golf course, but it was also very cold. Liz nestled up to her dad and said, "I just need to know. Do you feel okay about David now?"

Ned laughed. "I'll never forgive him for telling me that he was rusty at golf before we played that day, but other than that, he's not so bad."

"Dad, be serious. You kept telling us that we weren't right for each other. You don't feel that way now, do you?"

Ned wasn't sure when he had changed his mind about that, but he knew what had caused him to start thinking differently about David. "Liz, you're the one who figured the boy out. He really does hunger and thirst after righteousness. Since you told me that, I've watched him, and everything about him seems to come under that heading. It also explains why he would gravitate to you."

"But does he still annoy you?"

"Well, you know, a little. But that's only because I'm such a wicked sinner. What about you?"

"What do you mean?"

"Doesn't he annoy you sometimes?"

"No!" But after a couple of seconds, she added, "Well . . . yeah. Sometimes. The other day he saw me chomping down this huge chunk of fudge. He didn't say anything, but I knew what he was thinking, so I made him eat some of it. That's my goal— to corrupt him. If I can't get up to his level, I'll try to pull him down to mine."

"Or even down to *mine*."

"Oh, sure. You say that. But I noticed when the candy was being passed around last night, you didn't even touch it."

"I know. But don't tell David that. I'm trying to sneak up on him while he's not looking. The other day I finally made it to the top of Snake Creek."

"I thought you did that a long time ago."

"Oh." *I can't believe I said that.* "Well, I may have given that impression. But now I *have* made it, and my next goal is not to crawl on my hands and knees the last hundred yards. I want to run it with David next summer and go so fast that I make him plead for mercy."

"Don't count on it. He still runs every morning, even with snow on the ground."

"I was afraid of that."

Liz put her arms around her dad's waist, and he wrapped his arm around her shoulders. "He really is good, Dad. He told you that he loses interest in things, but I've decided that's not true. I think he gets embarrassed at being better than everyone else, so he backs off. He doesn't want people to be uncomfortable around him."

"Liz, you know as well as I do, I was having trouble letting you go, and I took it out on him."

"I understand that better now. I think maybe I'm not so different." She put her cheek against his shoulder, apparently to warm it.

"Maybe we better go inside."

"I just want to tell you this one thing first. That afternoon when you came down to bring us the spare tire—oh, by the way, we need to bring that back to you, but David still hasn't tracked down his own spare."

Ned leaned his head back and laughed. "What a flake!"

"But that afternoon, after I went home, I felt really strange. It just seemed so weird to see you with someone who wasn't Mom. I had been telling you to ask Carol out, but then, when I saw you with her, it felt to me like you were doing something wrong."

"I know. I still feel those twinges sometimes."

"But I'm just saying, we both had things to adjust to."

"Of course."

"Have you kissed her yet?"

"Out of wedlock? Of course not. I hope you haven't kissed David either."

"You've been kissing her, haven't you?"

"That makes it sound like we sit around and make out all the time. I've kissed her exactly three times, not counting a little peck I just gave her at the door when she came in. Oh, and I guess you'd say that she's kissed me about that many times—when I didn't make the move." Liz laughed at that, and her breath blew steam past Ned's face. "But how do you feel about that?" Ned asked. "Are you still uncomfortable with the idea?"

Liz thought for a time before she answered. "Maybe a little. When I see you two together, it reminds me how much I miss Mom. But I really love Carol, and I've been praying a lot about her. I have the feeling Mom likes her. I think she's happy for you."

Ned hadn't been anywhere near tears, but suddenly he felt his eyes filling up. "All in all, I'd still rather have your mother back," he said.

"I know. Me too. But this is okay."

"Yeah. I think so. It's just sort of complicated. Carol does things a little differently from your mom—thinks a little different. That's okay, but it catches me off guard sometimes and knocks me out of my comfort zone. Then there's all the practical stuff—deciding about houses and putting families together and all that. I wonder, for instance, what Christmas will be like in years to come."

Liz pulled away and turned so she could look into her dad's face. "What are you saying, Dad? Have you already asked her to marry you?"

"No. But I'm sure that's coming. We've talked about all those things."

"I didn't think you would move that fast, Dad. Two weeks ago you were talking about 'going slow.'"

"I know. But life is starting to mean something again. That makes up for all the problems. I'm ready to quit playing and do some things I need to do."

"Have you decided what those things are?"

"Not entirely, but Carol and I want to serve some missions. I've got enough money, and we're young enough that we could go several times. She's got a good little business, but she runs it mostly on instinct. I'm going to develop a business plan for her and see if we can get the shop on really solid ground. Then she might sell it. Once she does, we'll probably put in our papers for our first mission."

"But what are you going to do in the meantime, while Carol's going off to Salt Lake every day?"

"I've thought a lot about that. I just can't face another year of skiing and golfing and pretending that I'm having fun. I've got to do something productive. There's a branch of Utah Valley State College over in Heber, and I've agreed to teach a class there. I'll probably go down with Carol to her store some days, too, and I've also decided to get serious about my family history research."

"That sounds good, Dad."

"I've been all wrapped up in myself these last two years, and that doesn't work. I've got to find ways to give something back." He laughed, softly. "There's one other thing I'm going to do. What do you think it is?"

"Uh . . . you're going to start an a cappella choir and go around singing at hospitals?"

"Well, no." He grinned. "But you're kind of close. I've thought about David's example, and I do want to do some volunteering. Since my grandkids are spread all over the world, and

I can't do much for them, I thought I'd try to help some other guy's grandchildren. I signed up to start tutoring at Midway Elementary."

"That's great!" Liz said. She was laughing with that mellow barking sound, taking a little more joy in this than Ned quite understood.

"What's so funny?"

"What you said. It sounds like you're trying to be more like David. I don't think I saw that one coming."

"No. I didn't either." But it struck Ned that it was true. He took Liz back into his arms and told her, "You and I are both going to learn some things from that boy."

"I know. I love him so much, Dad. But I want you to know, I'm finding out all kinds of little things wrong with him. He's not nearly so perfect as you thought he was."

"Good! Tell me every bad thing you discover. Before long he'll be like one of my own sons."

She tightened her grip, and they laughed together. "Everything's going to be okay, Dad. I think things are turning out the way they're supposed to."

"If Carol and I do get married, will it bother you to come home and see her here with me?"

Liz stepped back and looked at him. "At first it will, I guess. I don't know. But it's better than going away to med school and leaving you here alone."

Ned nodded, and he thought about all the adjustments. At times it seemed more than he was ready for. But he told Liz, "If I can't jump over the fence, I'll just scramble through it the best way I can. That's what we'll both have to do."

"That's right," Liz said. "But let's go inside. I'm freezing."

"Go ahead. I'll come in just a minute."

When Liz turned toward the house, Ned turned too, and he noticed that David was standing on the other side of the glass doors. When David saw Liz walk toward him, he opened the door and stepped outside. "Were you two having a little chat?" he asked.

"Yeah. But it's too cold out here. Let's talk in the house."

"Okay," David said, but he didn't follow Liz inside immediately. He closed the door behind her, and then he said, "Ned, I watched you two out here, and it was hard for me. I feel like I'm a thief running off with your daughter."

"It's okay. You can have her. I'll trade you for my spare tire."

"Oh, yeah. I've got to get that back to you."

"Yes, you do. You've got to get your life in order, young man. I see some real signs of irresponsibility."

David smiled, but he said, "There is something kind of sad about the way life always has to change. I look forward to having kids, but I can already imagine how hard it is when they leave home."

"That's what parents tell their kids. The truth is, we can't wait." But Ned couldn't manage a laugh. He looked away from David, toward the windows, saw his sons in the kitchen, Liz there with them now. "It *is* hard, David, but the only thing worse would be if things didn't change."

"Yeah." David tucked his hands into his pants pockets. "Are we okay with each other now, Ned?"

"Not if you keep asking me pretty little questions like that. I'm from the old generation. When we want to tell a guy he's all right, we just give him a punch in the shoulder, and maybe grunt. We don't use any words."

David nodded, smiling bigger.

"Actually, David, I need to apologize. I made things too tough on you, and I'm sorry about that."

"Well, you just—"

"I was jealous of you. And it wasn't just about golf. You're thirty years younger than I am, and yet you're farther along than I am when it comes to living the way we all should."

"No. That's not true, Ned. The fact is, you and I are a lot alike—more than I think you've ever noticed. Everything is an effort for me. I'm trying to live the way I should, but it's a struggle for me. For you, it's just the way you are."

"Oh, please. Don't flatter me. You know what a reprobate I am."

"No you're not, Ned. You're as good a man as I know. For one thing, you're a great father."

Ned didn't think so, but David seemed serious, and Ned hardly knew what to make of that. He couldn't think of a single thing to say.

Then David stepped forward, and for a moment Ned almost panicked. He didn't want to hug the guy—not out here all alone. But David knew what to do. He doubled up his fist, gave Ned a fairly decent punch in the shoulder, and made a little grunt. Ned laughed, and then he did the same to David. They nodded to each other, resolutely, and the moment would have been perfect if David hadn't had tears in his eyes. At least the boy knew when to get away. He walked back into the house without saying another word.

Ned was freezing, but he stayed out in the cold. He turned around, looked out across the snow, and he stood with his arms wrapped across his chest. Overall, it seemed that things were working out well, but it was Christmas Eve, and underneath his satisfaction was still a longing that hadn't gone away. He wanted to talk to his wife.

*Kate, I know you don't really talk to me. But I hope this*

*is all right with you, what's happening. I wish that you could at least tell me that much.*

But the night remained silent and silver. The snow muffled all sound, and Ned felt the quiet powerfully, like the silencing of the voice he had clung to so long.

He was about to step back inside to his family when he saw a movement along the tree line just beyond the near fairway. Then he realized that it was a deer, a doe by herself, that had seemingly appeared out of nowhere. It stood for a moment, then looked across the snow toward him, as though it were seeing Ned. The two watched one another for a time before the deer turned and walked through the snow, lifting its feet high, until it disappeared into the shadows behind the trees. Ned didn't know what significance to find in this quiet appearance in the moonlight, tonight of all nights, but he felt it as one more gift.

"Good-bye," he said. "You go ahead."

At that same moment he heard the door open, and he turned to see Carol step outside. She looked pretty in her Christmas dress, and she came to Ned and put her arms around him. "Are you okay?" she asked.

"Yes," he said.

"You miss her tonight, don't you?"

"Yes. But it's okay. Everything's okay."

"I couldn't love you if you didn't miss her."

Ned held Carol tight, clung to her. This wasn't perfect, not at all what he had expected out of life. But it was good. He was in the right place at the right time, and he was okay. God had apparently brought him to this beautiful place—even if the trip hadn't been the one he would have chosen for himself.

# CHILDREN OF THE PROMISE

*The bestselling World War II series by Dean Hughes*
*Experience the "Greatest Generation" in a whole new way!*

 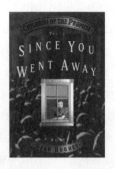 

Documentaries on World War II tell us what happened during that tremendous era of conflict and patriotism, sacrifice and heroism. But this gripping series of novels shows us how those experiences felt to those who lived them. You'll meet the Thomases, a Latter-day Saint family in Sugar House, just south of downtown Salt Lake City, Utah, and immediately be swept into their lives on the homefront as well as on the front lines in Europe and the Pacific. See for yourself why readers lined up each year for the next novel in the series!

**More than 600,000 copies sold in these two series!**

# HEARTS
## OF THE
# CHILDREN

*The saga of the Thomas family continues!*
*Meet a fascinating array of characters whose trials mirror our own*

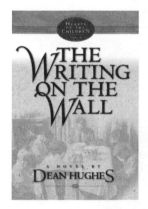  

The turbulence of civil unrest and brooding war. The increasing temptations of the world. The struggle over conflicting priorities in a time of unprecedented freedom from restraint. In so many ways, the 1960s ran on a course astonishingly parallel with our own day. As the Thomas grandchildren come into their adult years, the lessons they learn resonate in our hearts—for they are the timeless lessons of love, family, and courage to stand by our convictions.

*Publishers Weekly* calls Dean Hughes
a "masterful, epic storyteller"!